CHASING SHADOWS

ALASKA COZY MYSTERY #6

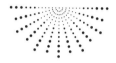

WENDY MEADOWS

MAJESTIC OWL PUBLISHING LLC

CHAPTER ONE

Sarah spotted movement in the backyard. She carefully pulled back the curtain covering the kitchen window and peered outside, expecting to see a fox, a raccoon, maybe even a bear; after all, it was spring, and animals were out prowling around for food. But instead of spotting a fox or a bear roaming around her green backyard, Sarah spotted a small puppy wandering around, lost and confused. "Oh," she exclaimed quickly, in a motherly tone, and dashed out of the kitchen door and around the side of her cabin into the backyard. "Puppy...puppy," she called out in a sweet, warm, loving voice.

The puppy paused, looked up, and spotted a woman walking across the yard wearing a dress the same color as the clear sky soaring above. The woman didn't seem threatening and her voice sounded gentle and kind. So the puppy did what all scared, lost, and hungry puppies do: it crouched down and began whining. "It's alright," Sarah soothed the puppy as she approached slowly, in a non-threatening manner so as not to scare the puppy away. "My, aren't you beautiful, too." The puppy wagged its bushy black and white tail. Sarah smiled, stopped a few feet from the puppy and bent down. "You look like...yes...a husky. Oh, yes, look at those bright blue eyes."

The puppy stared at Sarah and let out a hungry little bark. Sarah smiled. "Are you hungry?" The puppy slowly wagged its tail again. "I take that as a yes," Sarah said and stared at the beautiful puppy. The last thing she expected before lunch was to find a lost puppy in her backyard. She searched the puppy for a collar but didn't locate one. "No collar...no tags...well, you seem to be lost," she said and carefully eased forward. "I'm going to pick you up, okay? Don't be afraid." The puppy watched Sarah with careful eyes. Sarah smiled and gently took the puppy into her arms. "My, you can't be more than...five or six weeks old," she smiled down into the puppy's sweet face. "Now where did you come from?" The puppy stared up into Sarah's bright and loving eyes and simply wagged its tail. Sarah nuzzled the puppy on its nose and then, very carefully, checked its gender. "You are a...girl. Oh, yes you are." The puppy wagged her tail.

Sarah carefully walked back into the kitchen and placed

the puppy down onto the wooden floor. "Let me get you some milk...and...something soft...maybe a can of tuna fish." Sarah hurried over to the kitchen cabinets and retrieved two brown bowls small enough for the puppy to eat and drink from. She filled one bowl with milk and the other with tuna fish, and sat the bowls down next to the kitchen table. The puppy, excited to see food, waddled over to the bowls, sniffed the milk and then the tuna fish, and then looked up at Sarah as if waiting for permission to eat. "Go ahead, eat, girl." The puppy wagged its tail and began lapping up some milk.

As the puppy drank her milk, Sarah heard Conrad's truck pull into her driveway. She quickly ran her fingers through her hair, brushed the front of her dress, and hurried to start a pot of coffee, feeling like a nervous schoolgirl. Why? She didn't know. Despite all the adventures they had shared, she wasn't romantically involved with Conrad and she knew—deep inside of her heart—that diving into a serious relationship was far, far down the road. Yet, she felt nervous and excited as she scooped coffee grounds from a green coffee can. Conrad was a good man who cared for her, and lately, her thoughts seemed to be more on him—and even though she didn't know it, Conrad's thoughts were always on her. "Coffee, lunch, small talk, nothing else," Sarah whispered to herself as Conrad knocked on the back door. "Come in, the door is open."

Conrad opened the back door and stepped into the

kitchen wearing his usual leather jacket. When he spotted Sarah standing next to the coffee pot, he stopped in his tracks. Never in his life had he seen a woman so beautiful. He stared at Sarah as if she were a priceless dream sent down from heaven. "Uh...hi," he said and quickly looked down to hide his emotions. The last thing he wanted to do was make Sarah feel uncomfortable. "A puppy?" he asked.

"Oh, yes," Sarah said and blushed a little. The way Conrad looked at her, well, made her feel like a woman, and the feeling was nice. "I found her just a few minutes ago in the backyard. Poor thing seems to be lost."

Conrad closed the back door and looked down at the puppy. The puppy glanced up at Conrad, looked at Sarah, and then waited. "Go ahead, girl, drink your milk," Sarah smiled. The puppy, hearing Sarah's sweet voice, went back to her milk. "She doesn't have a collar," Sarah explained as the smell of hot, delicious coffee filled the kitchen air. "I didn't spot the momma, either."

Conrad rubbed his chin. "You might not find the mother at all," he said in a serious voice. Sarah frowned. "Sarah, a female husky was hit and killed by a reckless teenager this morning. The dog didn't have any tags or collar, either." Conrad sighed. "I know dogs, and I could tell the husky was milking a litter of pups. The husky was killed not too far from here, either."

"Oh, how horrible," Sarah said in an upset voice.

"Yeah, it is," Conrad agreed. He looked down at the puppy. "This little girl most likely belongs to the husky that was struck and killed. Could be more of them wandering around, too."

Sarah bit down on her lower lip. Snow Falls, Alaska didn't have a dog pound, and even if it did, she surely wouldn't take the puppy to a cold, unfriendly, scary building where it would be locked up in a cage. "Oh dear, what to do?" she asked.

Conrad looked over at Sarah and read the distress in her eyes. "Looks like you have a new roommate."

Sarah eased her eyes up to Conrad and then lowered them back down to the puppy. The puppy stopped drinking her milk and looked up at Sarah. Sarah couldn't help but to smile. "Well, girl, it looks like you and I are going to have to learn how to share a pillow." The puppy wagged her tail and began working on the tuna fish.

Conrad folded his arms together with a smile. "You're a real softie."

Sarah continued to stare at her new puppy. "She needs a home," she told Conrad, "and a mother."

"And you need a friend," Conrad added. "No, more than a friend...you need something to love."

Sarah stood silent and let Conrad's words soak into her mind. Did she need something to love? The answer was yes. Living alone in her cabin made her feel very lonely at times, no matter how many friends she knew in town. Having a sweet new puppy to love and take care of would be a blessing. "I guess I do," she smiled.

Conrad's grin widened. "So, what are you going to name her?" he asked.

"Oh, goodness," Sarah said and began to think. "Picking out a name for her might take some time, Conrad."

"Maybe not," Conrad replied. "How about Mittens?"

"Mittens?" Sarah asked, confused.

"Her paws," Conrad said and pointed out the puppy's white paws.

Sarah looked at the puppy's paws. "Oh...why, yes, her paws do look like little white mittens, don't they?" Sarah beamed. "Okay, Mittens it is."

Mittens stopped eating her tuna fish, glanced up at Sarah, wagged her tail, and then went back to eating. "I think she likes her name," Conrad laughed. "And speaking of names, where is Amanda? I thought she was going to join us for lunch?"

"My dear friend called and canceled on me," Sarah sighed. "Deliberately, of course, because she knew you were coming. And presumably..." Sarah trailed off, embarrassed.

Conrad chuckled and shook his head. "That woman is determined to play matchmaker."

"I know," Sarah agreed. "I was thinking we could have lunch at the diner in town. But now that Mittens is here...how about a turkey sandwich and a bowl of soup?"

"Sounds good to me," Conrad said happily. He liked spending time alone with Sarah at her cabin. The cabin felt like a place he could call home. Not that the cabin itself was special, but because Sarah made the cabin special.

Sarah pointed down at Mittens. "A third for lunch," she said and laughed. "Oh my, Conrad, what do I know about raising a puppy? There's...let's see...visits to the veterinarian's office...shots...potty training...puppy food to buy...toys...walks..." Sarah laughed again. "Mittens may look small now, but someday she's going to grow up, and in the meantime, her appetite is going to increase."

"Yeah, huskies have good appetites," Conrad agreed.

"I—" Sarah began to speak but stopped when the phone hanging beside the refrigerator rang. "I better answer that." Sarah walked over to the phone and answered the call. "Hello?"

"Sarah, darling, this is me, Rebecca," a raspy, smoky voice said. It was her literary agent.

"Oh, hello Rebecca," Sarah said and tensed up a little, even though her book sales were steady and strong and her new book was right on schedule.

Rebecca leaned back in a fancy desk chair and studied her expensive Los Angeles office. "Darling, nothing is wrong. I'm calling because I have fabulous news for you. Are you sitting down?"

Sarah made a strange face at Conrad. Rebecca never called unless she had a complaint or two. The woman was tough and all business until she warmed up to you; even then, she was hard as nails when it came to deadlines and never liked delays. But for whatever reason, Rebecca was very fond of Sarah and treated the woman like she was her own daughter. "I'm actually standing up."

"Well," Rebecca smiled and waved a smelly cigarette in the air with her right hand, "you might want to sit down, darling."

Sarah made a strange face again. Rebecca was an eccentric woman who was a throwback, a woman who never left the 1940s. The glitz and the glamor of LA and Hollywood show business was her favorite thing, outside of her work representing authors like Sarah. Rebecca loved theatrics and never delivered good or bad news without a bit of a performance. Obviously, Rebecca was preparing one of her signature theatrical announcements. "Rebecca, what is it?"

"Darling, a major studio has informed me that they wish to buy the rights to your books and begin transforming them into works on the big screen," Rebecca explained in a voice that soared with fantastic drama. "Darling, we're talking about more money than you can spend in Paris during a month of Sundays."

Sarah nearly dropped the phone. She was aware that her book sales were very strong and that her fan base was growing, but she never dreamed that anything she wrote would be brought to life on the big screen. "I'm..." she began to speak but stopped and looked at Conrad. Tears began falling from her eyes. "Rebecca...this is amazing news! I know...I mean, I know this winter was tough and I fell behind schedule some, and—"

"Oh, pish posh," Rebecca said, waving Sarah's comment away. "Darling, we all hit a snag every now and then. Now you listen to Rebecca. I need you in my office next Wednesday at eleven o'clock sharp. Mrs. Diane Samton is going to meet us with all the necessary paperwork and contracts."

"Next Wednesday...today is Tuesday—"

"My girl knows her days of the week, good," Rebecca said and continued without losing focus on the business at hand. "Darling, Mrs. Samton is representing a major studio that wants to set you up for life. I need your tush on a plane and in my office next Wednesday at eleven sharp."

"Of course," Sarah promised. "I'll be in Los Angeles next Wednesday and have my backside planted in your office at eleven sharp, Rebecca. Uh, may I ask which studio is interested in me?"

"That's a surprise."

"Oh...okay. Well, I guess I'll find out when I arrive in Los Angeles."

Rebecca beamed. "That's my girl," she said and eased off the accelerator a bit. "I was worried living in the woods and snow might have dented your mind. A good dose of the city will be good for you, darling." Rebecca paused and then said carefully, "Maybe a good dose of the city might convince you to move back home?"

Sarah looked at Conrad and then down at Mittens. "I am home, Rebecca," she promised. "I'm also very excited. I may not sleep a wink tonight."

"Me neither," Rebecca smiled and took a puff from her cigarette. "Darling, time is money. I'll see my girl next Wednesday. And after our meeting with Mrs. Samton, I'm going to take you out for a night on the town! Oh, it's going to be fantastic. Bye-bye for now."

Sarah hung up the phone and turned around. She felt giddy. "I have to be in Los Angeles next Wednesday."

"I heard," Conrad said with curiosity in his voice. "Good news?"

"The best, actually," Sarah confessed. She felt as if she was going to explode inside. And then she did. "Oh, Conrad," she exclaimed and ran over to him and hugged him as tightly as she could, happy tears cascading down her cheeks. "A studio wants to turn my books into movies!"

"Hey, wow," Conrad said, a little shocked that Sarah was hugging him and crying at the same time. "Sarah, that's great. Really, that's big-time."

Sarah wiped at her tears and looked into Conrad's eyes. "I never dreamed this could happen," she confessed. "This past winter was so hard...I barely caught up on my writing...and now spring is here and the flowers are blooming," she said in a dreamy voice. "The hard winter has passed."

"And you're happy," Conrad said, looking deep into Sarah's eyes.

"Yes," Sarah replied and hugged Conrad again. For a moment, she rested in Conrad's embrace and closed her eyes. But before she allowed herself to become too comfortable, she pulled away. "I better call Amanda and tell her to start packing," she said and ran back to the phone.

Conrad smiled. It was great to see Sarah so happy. "I guess I'll slip away and go get a bite at the diner. It looks like you're going to be very busy for the rest of the day."

Sarah spun around and looked at Conrad. "Oh no, you don't," she said. "You go home and start packing, too. I'm not going to Los Angeles with just Amanda. Besides, I want you to meet Pete...oh, Pete, it's going to be so great seeing him again."

"You...want me to go?" Conrad asked with surprise.

"Please," Sarah said, turning the full force of her happiness on him. "Conrad, I love Amanda, but someone has to babysit her while I'm in my meeting."

Conrad sighed. "Sarah, I don't have any more free days," he said, reluctant to disappoint her. "I'm tied to the office for a while. But," he said, "I can take care of Mittens for you while you're gone."

Sarah felt her heart break a little. However, she understood. The life of a cop was never an easy one. "Let's go have lunch at the diner, on me."

"What about Mittens?"

Sarah smiled at her new friend. "I'll bring my girl along. Both of them." She hurried to call Amanda and tell her best friend the good news and to invite her to the diner with them, while Mittens licked at the last bits of tuna fish in the bowl and wagged her tail happily to see her new friend so happy.

―――――――――

Amanda watched Mittens sniff around a sleepy green field, resting in the breeze of a late, lazy evening. "Where are we, anyway?" she asked Sarah. Their road trip had come to an unexpected halt.

Sarah leaned back against her jeep and folded her arms. "Maybe it was a mistake to drive," she whispered in a miserable voice. "We're lost. My jeep has a flat tire. It's getting dark and Mittens can't seem to make up her mind whether she is going to do her business or not." The puppy romped through the flowers and the tall grasses, unconcerned.

Amanda glanced toward the blazing red western sky. Images from old horror movies began to play in her mind. "Two beautiful women stranded on the side of a desolate road...one dressed in a lovely pink and white dress...the other," Amanda looked at Sarah, "well, wearing a simple gray dress...but style doesn't matter to a hungry killer. All the killer cares about is―".

"June Bug, please," Sarah begged, "enough with the drama. I am a retired detective who is carrying a concealed weapon. We may be lost, but we're not helpless." Sarah watched Mittens finally make a quick tinkle. "Good girl."

Amanda watched Sarah walk into the field to retrieve the furry little husky. Mittens wagged her tail and licked Sarah in the face. "Oh, she's a sweet little critter," Amanda said and then looked up at the sky again. "Too bad she isn't a vicious attack dog. What we need right about now is a German shepherd, love."

Sarah placed Mittens gently into the front passenger seat of her jeep, rolled down the window, and closed the door. Mittens, tired from her romp in the field, quickly plopped down on the soft blanket Sarah had placed there for her. The little puppy seemed to love the jeep—the comforting smell of Sarah was all around her—and felt secure enough to drop off into an easy sleep, without fear of outside threats. "She's going to sleep," Sarah told Amanda and gently patted Mitten's head. "Sleep, sweet baby."

Amanda looked to her right. All she saw was a very long, two-lane back road surrounded in places by thick woods and open fields in turn. She looked to her left and saw more of the same. "You're not upset with me, are you, love?"

Sarah wanted to be upset with Amanda for suggesting they get off the main road for a little sight-seeing adventure. But Sarah sighed, remembering that she had agreed to it and even supported the idea. After all, it was only Sunday and there was plenty of time to spare before her appointment with Mrs. Samton. Besides, she needed a long, open road to think on. "No, I'm not mad at you, June Bug. I agreed to leave Alaska early and drive to Los Angeles instead of flying."

"I know, love, but it was my idea to have a road trip, just us girls," Amanda replied guiltily. "We could be in Los Angeles right now, resting our tired feet in a luxurious suite and distracting our worried minds with delicious room service."

Sarah looked at Amanda. Amanda's face was wrinkled with worry and guilt. "Oh, come now," she said and patted Amanda's hand, "we can't let a little flat tire stop our road trip, can we? Besides, we know we're in Oregon, so we're not really lost, are we?"

"Well...yes," Amanda agreed and gave Sarah a grateful smile.

"I admit that this little detour does have me worried," Sarah continued. "But my worry is irrational. I'm anxious to reach Los Angeles, June Bug, that's all." Sarah raised her eyes to the western sky. "I'm anxious to see Rebecca."

"I can tell," Amanda told Sarah in a caring voice. "I guess my nerves would be a bit frazzled if I was meeting with someone from a big movie studio. Do you have any guesses who it is?"

Sarah bit her lip, reluctant to say the next part. "I didn't at first. But Rebecca called me back with some...other news, and told me the studio name. J&P Brothers."

"J&P Brothers is a famous studio!" Amanda's eyes went wide with surprise. But she could see that her friend was not excited. It was clear that a sharp splinter was sticking into her friend's heart. "Okay, spill the beans. I wasn't going to say a word, but look at you. You were okay up until this morning's phone call from Rebecca. But you've been on edge ever since then. That's why I suggested this little detour, love. Not to cause trouble, but to help. I was worried about you and thought seeing a bit of lovely countryside might calm your nerves."

Sarah glanced down the deserted road. There wasn't a car in sight. "I know you care," Sarah promised Amanda and studied the landscape. "We may have to see some of this lovely countryside on foot."

"We'll do more sightseeing in a minute. Start talking," Amanda ordered Sarah. "What did Rebecca say that has your nerves walking on a high wire, love?"

Sarah focused her attention on the front right tire. It was flatter than a pancake ran over by a steamroller. "I have a spare but can't find the jack...real smart, huh?"

"We'll talk about the jack later. Talk," Amanda demanded. She reached out and took Sarah's hand. "Love, what's eating at you? What did Rebecca tell you?"

Sarah stared into Amanda's concerned eyes. Amanda

wasn't going to back away. She dipped her head, drew in a deep breath, and said: "June Bug, a few years ago there was a murder at J&P Brothers studios. A young stuntman was found dead on a deserted back lot." Sarah looked in the jeep's window to check on Mittens. Mittens was sound asleep. "Jacob and Phillip Portland, the two brothers who own the studio..." Sarah paused and went silent.

"Don't leave me hanging," Amanda begged. "Keep talking, girl."

Sarah closed her eyes. In her mind, she saw the shadowy, deserted backlot filled with old buildings and dusty props, with the echoes of forgotten voices roaming on the wings of dry memories, never to be seen again. "Jacob and Phillip Portland became hostile toward the investigation," Sarah finally continued. "The movie the stuntman was working was in trouble. The production cost was skyrocketing, the director had been fired and replaced, the main female actor was threatening to quit, and to make matters worse, the film wasn't poised to do well in the theaters. As a matter of fact, the film was predicted to be a complete flop. And the murder investigation threatened to hold the whole production up, for months. Because so much money had already been invested, Jacob and Phillip Portland were bound to replace some of the money they invested into the film, no matter how little."

"Some is better than none, huh, love?"

"Better a seventy-percent loss than a ninety-percent loss," Sarah explained and rubbed her shoulder. "In the end, Jacob and Phillip Portland finally pulled the plug on the movie and accepted their losses after the press had a field day over the murder."

"A murder you were in charge of solving," Amanda guessed.

Sarah nodded. "A murder I never solved," she confessed. "The stuntman was strangled to death. No witnesses. No fingerprints. No weapon. No nothing. It was a clean murder." Sarah cast her mind back. "I chased down every possible lead I could find but I kept firing blanks." Sarah shook her head in disgust. "It seemed that Jacob and Phillip Portland ordered anyone who cared to be in show business to put a lock on their tongues. Eventually, I had to toss the case into the cold files and leave it alone."

"And now the same studio that caused a stain on your career wants to buy your books," Amanda said.

"The Portland Brothers must realize by now that the books they're about to turn into movies are written by the same detective who hounded their people over the death of an innocent man. Oh, I should have forced Rebecca to tell me which studio was wanting to buy my books when she first called me. I would have never dreamed a studio like J&P Brothers..." Sarah rubbed her eyes again. "Talk

18

about irony. I'm selling books about murder to a studio that still has an unsolved murder on its hands."

Amanda wasn't sure what to say. She saw the irony in the situation, but she also saw a deep worry in her friend. "Love, are you thinking...that the involvement of J&P Brothers is not a coincidence? That you're being lured back to Los Angeles as a ruse?"

"You read my mind well, June Bug," Sarah told Amanda. "My gut knows that Jacob and Phillip Portland would burn a piece of paper with my name on it if they found it, never mind my books. I'm anxious to get to Los Angeles and get to the bottom of this mystery."

"Do you think...Jacob and Phillip Portland might try and...kill you?" Amanda asked, her face clouded with worry.

Sarah looked up at the sky. "No," she answered honestly. "The Portlands are businessmen, not killers. But something isn't right in Tinsel Town, June Bug, if they were able to silence those witnesses. My gut is telling me I'm being lured back into town under false pretenses."

"So...does this mean you're not going to be a spoiled millionaire?"

Sarah hesitated to answer. She had been so excited at the idea of a studio buying her books. But now her excitement was replaced by worry and anxiety. "Right now, all I want to do is get to the bottom of this. Could it be there is absolutely nothing suspicious? Maybe. Then again, it could be that the file on this cold case has been reopened without me knowing, and that's why they're looking for me." Sarah looked up and down the road, shaking her head to clear her thoughts. "I thought getting off the main road would help me clear my mind. But being stranded like this is only making my mind work overtime."

"It is kinda spooky out here, isn't it? I keep expecting to see some horrible creature walk out of the woods, or some hitch hiker wearing a creepy clown mask," Amanda shivered. She wrapped her arms around her shoulders and glanced around. "Can't you just picture creepy banjos out in these Oregon woods? You don't think there's crazy people out here, do you? I mean, the last town we passed was a mere speck in the road...and that was a good ten miles back down the road, love." Amanda tilted her head north.

"I'm going to go crazy if you don't stop filling my mind with images of scary clowns and whatnot," Sarah fussed. "June Bug, this is Oregon. We're not being stalked by a bunch of crazy hillbillies playing banjos."

Amanda wasn't so sure. But before she could state her opinion she heard a sound in the distance. She popped forward, threw her hands to her eyes, and peered north and spotted an approaching truck. "Please don't be a crazy hillbilly clown...please don't be a crazy hillbilly clown...oh, please don't be a crazy hillbilly clown playing a banjo."

Sarah rolled her eyes and began waving her arms in the air. A minute later, a blue truck pulled up to Sarah. An older black man stuck his head out of the driver's side window. "What seems to be the problem?" he asked in a tired, patient voice.

"A flat tire," Sarah said and pointed at her jeep. "I have a spare but no jack."

The old man frowned as if not having a jack was a philosophical problem they agreed on. "Ain't got a jack myself, either. Ain't had a flat in over twenty years, though," he chuckled. "So now I don't see no sense in carrying one around every place I go."

Amanda looked at Sarah with worried eyes. "We can't get any cell phone reception out here, sir. Can you give us a lift into town?" she asked.

The old man chuckled again. "I can, but it won't do you no good. Old John will be closed up by now at the garage, he'll be home eating his supper with Paula, his wife of...oh, I'd say... about forty years now, give or take a year. Paula sure can cook up a good chili but can't bake a cake to save her life. Shame, too."

"Is there any twenty-four-hour towing assistance nearby?" Sarah asked in a calm voice. She knew becoming upset wouldn't do any good.

"Young lady, this here land you're driving through surrounds the little town of Prate. Prate sits way off on its own, too. Ain't another town in twenty miles of here. Interstate is a good ways off, too. So, ain't likely you're going to get a tow truck this far out, especially with it getting to supper time."

"My insurance covers twenty-four-hour roadside assistance," Sarah explained. "If I could just use your phone on the way into town, I could call—"

"Ain't got no phone," the old man said apologetically, "and I ain't going into town. I'm heading home for my supper and a nice sit on the front porch."

Amanda gave Sarah a desperate look. "We're stuck, then," she said and threw her arms up in the air. "We'll just have to wait and see if another person comes by."

"Ain't likely," the old man told Amanda, peering out the window at her in the twilight. "This here is the old farm road. Not many folks live off this road. Those who do have enough sense to be home eating supper by now."

"Then we're walking into town," Sarah told the old man and offered him a gentle smile. "I have to be in Los Angeles by Wednesday, sir. I don't have time to wait. I'll put my legs to good use. Thank you for stopping."

The old man stared at Sarah. He could tell by her eyes that as soon as he pulled off, she would take off for town on foot. "It'll be mighty dark by the time you get into town," he pointed out, troubled. "Town will be closed, too. The only payphone in town is outside the grocery store."

Amanda was crestfallen. She looked at the man despondently and her eyes were caught by a small, carved wooden cross hanging from the truck's rearview mirror. The old man saw her glance just then. He rubbed his chin, looked at Amanda and saw the gleam of hope in her eye, and then he rubbed his chin again. "Ain't right to leave two ladies stranded. No sir. If I did, my momma would tan my hide...if she could come down from heaven, that is."

Sarah felt hope rise in her chest. "Then you'll give us a ride into town?"

The old man hesitated and then slowly rubbed his head. "I reckon my supper is going to be late tonight," he said and tossed a thumb at the front seat. "You ladies crawl on in and I'll get my old truck turned around."

"Oh, thank you," Amanda erupted joyfully. She ran over to the old man, hugged his neck, and then kissed his cheek. "You're my hero!"

The old man blushed. "Ain't had a pretty lady kiss my cheek in years."

Sarah smiled and quickly woke Mittens. "Come on, girl, we have a ride."

The old man spotted Sarah gather the sleepy husky pup into her arms. "My, my," he said, "looks like we're going to have a full truck tonight."

Sarah quickly locked up her jeep and climbed into the front seat of the truck beside Amanda with Mittens in her arms. The man's face lit up with a warm smile, then he turned his truck around, and got it moving back toward town. The puppy looked at the old man and wagged its tail happily, as if it felt goodness in him and his old but sturdy truck. But Sarah couldn't help but feel like a bad storm might await them in town.

CHAPTER TWO

"*N*ame is Nate, by the way. Nate Ringgold."

Sarah leaned forward and glanced past Amanda at Nate. The old man had his left elbow stuck out of the driver's window and his left hand on the worn curve of the steering wheel. He was smiling, enjoying the late spring evening air that softly blew across his wrinkled face. It struck Sarah that Nate was at peace—at peace with himself, the world, and most important, judging from the cross hanging in his truck, the Lord. Nate didn't have a care in the world—except being late for supper, that is. Sarah felt an instant warmth and affection toward Nate and relaxed in the loving feeling peeking up from the ground in her heart and reaching for life. "I'm Sarah. This is my best friend Amanda. And the puppy is Mittens."

"Nice to meet you all," Nate smiled. However, behind his

smile, his mind was mighty bothered. Something in Sarah's eyes was sure worrisome. Of course, Nate knew enough to never bother with other folks' business; that's another lesson his momma taught him. But Nate couldn't help but wonder what was bothering the pretty woman holding the little puppy. And what about her friend? The other pretty woman spoke like she was kin to King Edward or Henry or whoever might have been king of England back in the old days. The woman with the English accent had worry floating around in her eyes, too. Nate kept his smile up while his eyes checked the rearview mirror again.

Sarah read Nate's eyes. "No one is chasing us, Mr. Ringgold," she said in a gentle tone.

Nate let out a chuckle. "You're good at reading old men," he told Sarah. "Man can't help to wonder what you two ladies are doing way out here on this old farm road looking like two worried cats about to step into a room full of rocking chairs."

"We took a little sightseeing tour," Amanda jumped in before Sarah could speak. "I thought seeing some lovely countryside instead of a lousy highway might do us some good. I...kinda got us lost, you see. And then we got a flat."

"Ain't no flat on a strange road can make two people worry the way you are," Nate said and eased off his smile.

"Old Nate has been around for seventy-eight years. He ain't no fool."

Sarah pulled Mittens to her chest and let the evening air blow in her hair. "Mr. Ringgold—"

"Call me Nate."

Sarah looked down into the puppy's sleepy face. Mittens raised her eyes and yawned. "Nate, I'm a retired detective from Los Angeles. I moved to Alaska to begin living a quiet life after my husband...divorced me. Long story short—"

"Long story short, my friend has been called back to Los Angeles because a major studio wants to buy her books and turn them into movies," Amanda blurted out.

"Oh, Amanda," Sarah moaned.

"Well, I'm proud that you're a successful writer, love. It makes my heart sad that you hide behind a penname instead of letting the world know who you are. But I understand why, and—" Amanda paused as she realized she had put her foot square in her mouth. "And I just blabbed to a stranger who you are. Oh, love, I'm so sorry."

Sarah patted Amanda's arm. "I know you care. And I doubt this stranger will try and track me down one day."

Nate pulled the conversation into his mind and chewed on it. "Being a cop must mean you made a lot of enemies," he said.

"Yes, sir," Sarah replied in a respectful tone. "That's why I write under a penname."

"Good enough for me," Nate said and cleared the fog out of the air only to bring in a rain cloud. "Seems like you got yourself some good news, but Old Nate don't see happiness in your eyes."

Sarah stared at the open fields rolling past her on the right. The countryside was beautiful, calm and sleepy. Unfortunately, her troubled heart refused to be settled by the tranquility before her. I'm being set up, Sarah thought to herself and scratched Mittens' ears for comfort. "I think there might be..." Sarah paused and bit down on her lip, looking at Amanda for help.

"We think there's a trap waiting for us in Los Angeles and this whole buying-the-book deal is a scam. Or it's the cheese to draw the mouse to the trap," Amanda finished for Sarah.

"Is that right?" Nate asked and shook his head. "Someone down there in the big city still got a grudge against you, huh?"

Sarah was a little surprised at Nate's calm tone but not surprised in the least at his sharp mind. "Could be that way, yes," she confessed. "I'm anxious to get to Los Angeles by Wednesday. I plan to arrive at the meeting location a little early and stake out the scene."

"Smart woman," Nate said and flicked on the headlights

with his left hand. A set of dim but reliable headlights tossed out two beams of light into the air. Then he glanced into the rearview mirror again. He spotted a pair of headlights racing down the road. "Well now, seems like we have some company."

Sarah spun around in her seat and spotted the headlights. Her stomach sank. "Take Mittens," Sarah told Amanda. Amanda quickly took Mittens and watched Sarah retrieve her gun. "Nate, speed up," she said.

Nate looked over at Sarah, saw her check the gun in her hand, and nodded. "Old Nate never did like breaking the speed limit, but he sure will now," he said and stomped on the gas pedal. The truck roared forward.

"Maybe it's just a bunch of teenagers out for a night ride?" Amanda said as her stomach tensed. "I mean, who in the world knows where we are, love?"

"Maybe my cell phone is being tracked?" Sarah suggested.

Amanda pulled Mittens closer. "Nate, go faster, if you can."

"This here old truck won't go no faster than sixty," Nate told Amanda, "but I'll sure get him to try. Come on old boy, cough up the dust and get moving."

Sarah glanced over her shoulder. The car was quickly

closing the gap. "Nate, when I give you the word, ease off the gas."

"What?" Amanda asked in a shocked voice.

"Let's find out if it's teenagers after all," Sarah replied tensely.

"Ain't no teenagers out this late in Prate," Nate objected. "I have been driving this road my entire life and ain't never seen any of our local kids making fools of themselves—well, not this late in the day, anyway."

Sarah focused on the car. She believed every word Nate told her, but she had to be sure. "Okay, Nate...get ready..." she said, watching the car zoom up behind the truck. "Okay now...slow down...not too much, though...just enough to make the car pass you."

Nate eased off the gas and let the truck drop down to a cozy twenty miles per hour. A gray BMW with dark tinted windows quickly overtook them, then swerved smoothly into the left lane, sped around the truck, then pulled back into their lane and slammed on its brakes so that they almost collided. "Hold on!" Nate yelled and with skilled hands and a calm mind, he steered the truck into the left lane and stomped on the gas. The truck sped past the BMW. As it did, Sarah cast her eyes at the license plate. "Where's that car from?" Nate asked.

"California tags," Sarah replied in a heavy voice as the

BMW got moving again, pursuing them. "Nate, this truck isn't going to outrun that BMW."

"Nope. But they're following us. And Old Nate isn't a fool," Old Nate said and pointed up the road with his left hand. "The Monroes live about a half mile ahead. If we can make it to their driveway, I'll swing in for a visit. Old George Monroe don't take nonsense off folks from out of state. He'll give this situation a helping hand."

Amanda fought back the urge to reach out and hug Nate. The old man sure was a diamond in the rough. "You show them, love!"

Before Nate could reply, the BMW pulled up even with the truck again, and to Sarah's horror, the driver's side window of the BMW rolled down. A rough, powerful hand appeared with a gun and began firing at the truck. "Get down!" Sarah yelled and threw her arms over Amanda's head. As she did, an image flashed in her mind: it was the isolated cabin belonging to the murdered real estate tycoon, a case she had worked on months ago. The outlines of the lonely cabin whispered into her mind. She saw the cabin sitting alone in the Alaskan wilderness, as if hungry for life to reenter its heart—longing for love and light, laughter and peace. Sarah wasn't sure why the cabin entered her mind when it did, and she sure didn't have time to psychoanalyze it in the moment, either. The sound of the gunshots quickly snapped her out of her reverie and chased the isolated cabin away. "Stay down," Sarah yelled again.

"Who is getting up, love?" Amanda shouted and pulled Mittens under her arms. "Hold on, sweet baby."

Nate narrowed his eyes and focused on the road. There was no sense in panicking—panicking only gets you killed. "Let Old Nate do the driving, ladies, and don't worry your little minds about missing supper."

Sarah moved into a crouch, planning to return fire, but hesitated. She only had the bullets sitting in her gun and one extra clip. She couldn't afford to blindly fire at a speeding vehicle and chance wasting bullets. Instead of firing, she kept her head low and waited for Nate to reach Mr. Monroe's driveway. When she felt Nate swing the truck into a dangerous turn, the tires scattering a plume of gravel and mud around them, she tilted her head up just in time to see the BMW race past the dirt driveway Nate had turned onto. The BMW slowed and then sped away as Nate tore down the driveway without looking back. "They're driving on," she said in a relieved voice.

Nate kept his foot on the gas pedal and didn't let up until he slammed the truck to a stop in front of a beautiful two-story farmhouse with a gorgeous wrap-around porch. Seconds later, a large man built like a grizzly bear stepped out onto the front porch carrying a double barrel shotgun. He squinted his eyes and studied Nate's truck. "Nate Ringgold, is that you?"

Nate eased open the driver's side door and waved his hand. "Yeah, it's me, George, so don't go blasting your gun at my empty belly."

Sarah looked at Amanda as they sat up in the truck. "Are you okay?"

"No," Amanda sighed. "I was really hoping for a fun, easy-going trip to Los Angeles, just us girls," she explained. "The trip is ruined now. Nevermind the bullets."

Sarah patted Amanda's arm and opened the passenger side door. "Come on, June Bug. Let's say hello to Mr. Monroe and let Mittens get some fresh air."

Amanda climbed out of the truck and looked at the farmhouse. The farmhouse was an absolute dream, built and expanded by generations of Monroes. The open fields behind the farmhouse smelled of sweet hay. If Amanda wasn't so scared she would have run up to the farmhouse and hugged it. Instead, she looked up at the darkening sky and saw the first star of the night appear. "It's going to be a long night," she whispered and set Mittens down at her feet.

"What's this all about, Nate?" George demanded. "You come racing down my driveway like a man on fire. You in trouble? I heard shooting."

Nate tossed a thumb at Sarah and Amanda. "I picked these here two pretty ladies up off the road when I saw them standing with their jeep that got a flat tire. Wasn't long before some fancy car with California plates came racing at us with guns blazing."

George gripped his shotgun with powerful hands. He was a large man who didn't tolerate nonsense. Being a God-fearing, hard-working and practical man were the three main tenets that guided his life. "Where is this car now, Nate?"

Nate tossed a thumb back down the driveway with a mischievous grin. "Sped off when I pulled a surprise turn into your lane. You might want to call the sheriff and get him out here, George. Me and the ladies will stand out here and keep watch."

George stared down the driveway and then walked back inside without saying a word. "Nice man," Amanda groaned.

"Can you blame him?" Sarah asked. "Put yourself in his shoes."

"I know, I know," Amanda apologized. "But he can put himself in our shoes, too. Someone is out to kill us...well, you. But that involves me, love. I'm not dancing on marshmallow clouds right now. And even worse, I need to visit the loo really, really bad...and I don't think Mr. Shotgun Man is going to let me use his bathroom."

Mittens didn't have a problem, however. She let out a happy stream next to Amanda. Amanda cried out when she realized what had happened and began shaking urine off her shoe. Nate shook his head at Amanda's noises and turned instead to study Sarah's shadowy face. "Them folks shooting at us, you know them?"

"I might," Sarah replied, feeling the night settle into her heart. "But I can't be certain if they are who I think they are, Nate. I have to be cautious in my thinking right now."

"Fair enough," Nate told Sarah. "I'm not in any hurry to find out who shot at us from that fancy car. I figure we'll know soon enough."

Sarah kept her eyes on the driveway. Surely, she thought, the BMW wouldn't dare return to attack on private property. An open road attack was the mode of operation for hired killers—quick and easy with no witnesses. Private property changed the rules of the game. Private property meant the possibility of prying eyes, extra witnesses, other factors that could be very damaging in a court of law. "Focus," Sarah whispered and walked her mind back through time. "Focus on the case."

Amanda was shaking a stern finger at the husky puppy, but then she looked at Sarah. "Are we still going to Los Angeles, love?"

"If we can," Sarah replied. "You don't have to come with me."

Amanda put her hand on Sarah's shoulder and stared

down the dusty driveway. "I've already been shot at and used as a fire hydrant. I'm pretty much broken in for this case," she told Sarah with a grin as they continued to wait for the local sheriff to arrive.

"A dead body?!" Sarah exclaimed, staring at the old man who wore his sheriff's uniform so baggy that the brown fabric hung on his frail body like a silly clown outfit.

Sheriff Paul Bufford was just as shocked as Sarah to find a dead body in the passenger seat of her jeep. He was an old man of seventy-one and not in the mood to be up so late dealing with "a bunch of horse manure," as he had muttered at first. This was one something that he just knew would interfere with his bedtime cup of apple cider and honey. "A woman," he said, and hitched up his uniform britches as a strong wind snapped at his thin gray hair and weathered face. "Someone called and left an anonymous tip about the body. I was already headed out here when dispatch called me about this car chase with gun shots by the Monroe place."

"Wasn't no dead body when I picked these two ladies up off the road," Nate said and shoved his hands down into the front pockets of his pants. "No sir, wasn't no dead body at all, Paul."

"Well, Nate, there's a dead body now," Paul fussed and

folded his arms together and looked at the front porch. "George, will you put that shotgun away, for crying out loud?"

"Not until you're off my property," George said, as the night wind ruffled the hem of his flannel work shirt around him. He pointed his shotgun at Sarah in a gesture. "This woman claims she's a retired detective from Los Angeles. You better check her story, Paul."

"Already ran her," Paul continued in a patient but slightly cranky voice. "I'm not stupid, George. I've been Sheriff for over twenty-two years now. Her name came up when I ran the vehicle registration and I called the place of employment listed as a reference in her old California DMV records." Paul focused his eyes on Sarah. "Ms. Garland is who she says she is."

Sarah caught the curious look in Sheriff Bufford's eye. "Who did you speak with in Los Angeles?" she asked.

"A man who seems to know you very well."

"Pete," Sarah said.

"That's the man," Paul agreed. "Your friend, Ms. Garland, wasn't too happy to hear about your side stop in my county, either. And I'm not too happy, either. There has never been a murder in or around Prate, Oregon before, never. Prate was listed as one of the top ten safest places for families to live in."

"In the 1962 Readers Digest," Nate threw the fact at Paul. Amanda exchanged a look with Sarah and suppressed a smile. This was evidently a long-standing dispute between the men.

"Doesn't matter when the year was, Nate," Paul argued. "The fact is, we have a murder on our hands and the peaceful reputation of Prate, Oregon has been changed for good."

"You said it was a woman's body you found?" Sarah asked.

"Yes, a woman," Paul snapped. He would rather be at home, and Nate Ringgold's irksome argument only served to make him miss his wife Sophia, who would be reading her usual Readers Digest by now. Instead, he was standing out on George Monroe's farm feeling a chill from the night air. "Ms. Garland, Prate is a small town. We have a hospital the size of a classroom and one single red light in town. Prate is a farming community filled with families, not wild snakes from big cities. Now, you listen to me and listen close. I don't know what's going on, but you better put your badge back on and get to the bottom of this mess and fast. Am I making myself clear?"

"I'm retired, Sheriff."

"Not anymore. I'm deputizing you and your friend here," Paul told Sarah in a stern voice. "I figure if you can catch a deadly serial killer, well, you can catch whoever killed that poor woman and shoved her into your jeep." Paul ran his hands through his gray hair. "Truth of the matter is, my guys just aren't smart enough...I believe that you have nothing to do with the murder, and I also believe you are the best person to solve it."

Sarah took Mittens from Amanda and cradled the puppy in her arms. "Sheriff, last winter was very difficult for me and my friend. We dealt with a lot of deadly people. We're both tired and this is just a fun trip to Los Angeles to relax and forget our worries—"

"And sign a very generous contract from a major studio," Amanda pointed out.

Sarah sighed. "Yes," she agreed. "Sheriff, I have to get to Los Angeles for a meeting. I don't have time."

"You'll make time," he replied stubbornly. "You know I would have to detain you as a witness anyway. The faster you solve this, the faster you can leave. You brought this trouble to town, you can solve it, too."

"Which leads me to ask you about the dead woman." Sarah braced herself. "Sheriff, what did this woman look like?"

Paul hesitated and saw Nate staring at him. "Go on, Paul, tell the woman what she wants to know if you want her to do your job for you," Nate told him.

"The woman," Paul said, "well, I can describe her like

this." Sarah listened as Paul gave a perfect description of Rebecca. Tears began falling from her eyes. "Do you know the woman?"

Sarah nodded through her tears. "I spoke to her this morning."

"But...Rebecca was in Los Angeles," Amanda said in confusion.

"Maybe not," Sarah replied. She handed the puppy to Amanda and wiped at her tears. "I called Rebecca on her cell phone because I couldn't reach her at the office. Could she have been out of town? She didn't imply that she was, though..."

"Oh dear," Amanda sighed, "this case is really getting complicated." She wondered what this meant for her best friend's contract with the movie studio. When she looked at Sarah, she could see that in her grief, she had no idea what to think, either.

Nate watched Sarah wipe her tears. The woman had a good, gentle heart about her that pleased his own heart. "Somebody is trying to frame you for murder."

"Maybe, but I don't think so," Sarah said and thought about the gray BMW. "I think it's a warning. I'm being warned to back off and stay out of Los Angeles. Or so it seems. I could be wrong."

"Let's say you're right. Who is sending the warning?" Paul queried, furrowing his wrinkled brow.

"I'm not sure yet," Sarah confessed. "Right now, Sheriff, my enemies are in different corners and I don't know who is throwing the punches."

"Well, maybe your friend Pete will. He's driving up to Prate as we speak," Paul told Sarah. "I indicated I was investigating a body in your vehicle, and he immediately said he would come here."

"Pete is on his way?" Sarah asked as butterflies gripped her stomach.

"That's right," Paul said and shook his head. "The body is being taken over to the county morgue in Lawsondale." Paul rubbed his eyes. "I found a purse in your jeep belonging to the dead woman too, along with some luggage I'm assuming belongs to you. Anyway, your jeep is being towed to the garage in town. You can pick it up tomorrow morning. Not much more we can do tonight—"

"Sheriff, the people who killed my friend are still on the loose. You need to set up roadblocks and—" Sarah began.

Paul held up his hand. "Ms. Garland, this is Prate, not Los Angeles. If I go sticking roadblocks up in the night, why, every person in town will be in a panic and come running with questions. No ma'am, nothing doing."

"Sheriff is right," Nate told Sarah. "Folks in Prate get

mighty jumpy when a fly gets in their ointment," he explained. He tossed a thumb at George. "See what I mean?"

Sarah looked at George Monroe. The man still stood on the porch. He was on edge and ready to shoot at the first shadow that moved. "I guess I do."

"If folks in Prate get jumpy, you'll have a hundred Georges running around looking for shadows that ain't there, but they might fire on flesh and blood, that is," Nate cautioned Sarah. "Best to wait until morning and see what happens."

"I want the both of you at the station house at nine sharp. I'll deputize you at that time. Your friend Pete should be here around that time, too," Paul said and walked over to a brown and white sheriff's car that looked like an antique. "Keep your wits about you—and your sidearm—in case your attackers come back during the night. We believe in 'standing your ground' here in Oregon, as I'm sure you know."

"Let's pray for a peaceful night," Nate told Paul and waved him off. The Sheriff climbed into his car and drove off down the gravel driveway. "You ladies best come and stay the night with old Nate. Ain't no sense in going into town this late."

"Do you have room?" Amanda asked Nate.

"I live in an old farmhouse by myself," Nate explained.

"It's about the size of this one here. I'm sure we can find room," he finished and tipped Amanda a wink.

Sarah looked at George Monroe, who was still standing on his porch ready to fire at anyone who might threaten his homestead. "Mr. Monroe, we wish to apologize for causing you so much distress tonight. But I have to plead with you to please refrain from speaking about tonight's events to anyone."

"What she is saying is if you go running your mouth, the people who killed that poor woman may pay you and your family a visit, George," Nate said in a very serious voice. "Now, we both know you can wrestle a grizzly bear down to the ground, but bullets are a whole different story. The men shooting at us earlier weren't using shotguns, if you catch my drift."

"Yeah, I catch your drift, Nate," George said in a gruff voice. "I served in the Marines for two years. I understand weaponry. You just make sure next time someone goes shooting at you, get them to follow you down my driveway so I can get a good aim at them," George added and then walked inside and slammed his front door shut.

"Come on," Nate sighed, "let's get home. My tummy is rumbling and my supper is waiting."

"I'm going to ride in the back of your truck, Nate," Sarah

explained. "If we have company I'll be able to take better aim."

"Suits me just fine," Nate told Sarah and climbed into the passenger seat of his truck. "Amanda, you and the puppy better ride up in the cab with me."

"Go on," Sarah urged Amanda and hurried into the back of Nate's truck. "I'll be fine."

"Okay," said Amanda, who made a pained face and then reluctantly jumped into the passenger seat with Mittens. Nate got his truck moving and managed to drive them to his farmhouse without any problems, even though he expected to see the gray BMW again.

"Ah, home sweet home," Nate said, turning off the main road and driving down a very long dirt driveway. A couple of minutes later, he pulled up to a large farmhouse glowing with bright lights; every light in the farmhouse was on. The farmhouse resembled George Monroe's farmhouse—even down to the wrap-around porch. Yet this farmhouse seemed different somehow.

"Very beautiful," Amanda gasped and jumped out of the truck. "Los Angeles, get the bugs out of your teeth and look at this lovely home."

Sarah stretched her arms and crawled out of the truck, relieved that the gray BMW had not decided to make a second appearance. She felt tired, hungry and ready for a good night's sleep, even though she doubted sleep would come easy. At least the sight of Nate's farmhouse provided her with some comfort. "You're an artist," she said, glancing around at sculptures made of metal, cement, stone and other materials, sitting in the shadows.

"Oh, not me," Nate smiled. "My wife was the artist. I was the farmer. The work sitting around this here front yard belongs to her, not me." Nate walked over to a beautiful little boy and girl carved out of wood. "When my wife was in her younger years...my, what her hands couldn't create," he said and patted the wooden sculpture with sad hands.

Sarah looked at Amanda. Amanda sighed. "So sad," she whispered.

Sarah nodded. "I know," she whispered back and took Mittens from Amanda. She buried her face into the soft fur at Mittens' neck, drawing comfort from the puppy's contented snuffles.

Nate patted the wooden sculpture once more and then walked away. "I live off my social security and retirement now," he explained. "I knew someday I wouldn't be able to farm my land anymore so I put back money each month, even when food was tight on the table." Nate pointed to his house. "Worked real hard to pay off this here house and land, too. Now I'm just waiting to say goodbye to it someday and go on home and be with Jesus. I reckon this land is getting tired of seeing my old face," Nate managed to chuckle. "When the Good Lord says it's my time, then I'll say my goodbyes and go on home to my real home. This here old earth is just a strange place without my wife, even though at times it can seem very familiar. But, the seasons come and go and this old earth grows older by the day, just like you and me."

Amanda walked up to Nate and took his hand. "Before you're called home to Jesus, I'd like the privilege to know you more." She smiled into his kind face and felt peaceful. "Now let's go inside and eat. I'm starving."

"The pinto beans and cornbread might be a bit late tonight, but better late than never," Nate said and walked Amanda up onto the front porch. Sarah stood still in the night for a couple of minutes and listened to the stars whisper back and forth and the insects chatter. She felt a sweet peace walk up and stand next to her—a peace that she sometimes felt in Alaska when standing all alone in her kitchen, staring out into the backyard watching the snow fall with a warm cup of coffee in her hand. She loved the snow. She loved the way it seemed to carry her heart away into a wonderful and mysterious place that the world couldn't touch or harm. Sarah figured Nate felt the same about his farm. "You coming?" Nate called out.

"I'll walk Mittens first and then come inside," Sarah promised. Nate nodded and held open the door for Amanda.

Sarah drew in a deep breath, looked down at Mittens, and forced a smile onto her worried face. "Well, girl, you sure didn't sign up for this trip, did you?" The puppy made a tiny grunt and Sarah kissed Mittens on her nose. "I wish we were back home in our cabin together having a nice cup of coffee for me and a nice cup of warm chicken broth for you. But," Sarah said and coaxed Mittens over to a patch of field, "we have work to do before we can go home." Mittens looked up at Sarah and then stretched her eyes up to the stars. The world sure was a strange place.

CHAPTER THREE

*N*ate dipped a wooden spoon into a metal pot full of simmering pinto beans. "Beans and cornbread," he said, and smiled the way only an old-timer could, "sure fills the stomach well."

Sarah watched Nate stir the beans and looked around an open, vintage kitchen that felt soothing and warm. If she didn't know any better, Sarah would have sworn she had stepped back into the 1930s. The entire farmhouse felt like that. The furnishings, floors, and walls were authentic and not covered over with the kind of modern, cheap materials that greedy companies sometimes passed off as a substitute for old-fashioned integrity and workmanship. "I love your kitchen," she told Nate.

"My wife loved this old kitchen, too," Nate replied and continued to stir the beans. "Yep, my wife spent a good deal of time standing right where I'm standing, cooking up a storm." Nate chuckled to himself. "Poor soul always did burn the cornbread, but I never made a fuss of it."

Sarah smiled and closed her eyes. In her mind, she saw a beautiful young woman pulling a burned pan of cornbread out of the oven and a handsome young man, tired from the fields, leaning against the back door and shaking his head but not saying a word. "You and your wife shared a very special love, didn't you?"

"Still do," Nate told Sarah and set the wooden spoon in his hand down on a brown plate. "My wife may be in Heaven resting with Jesus, but just because she's gone from me doesn't mean the love we have for one another was buried under the ground. No ma'am," Nate said in a happy voice, "my wife is just waiting for this old man to join her in the Father's Kingdom is all. Why, that old woman is up there free as a bird and more alive than you and me are right this second. She's just waiting, like me, that's all."

Sarah sighed. The love Nate had for his wife touched her heart very deeply. "How did you meet your wife?" she asked.

"Yeah," Amanda jumped in excitedly. "Spill the beans, Nate and tell these two weary gals a sweet love story."

Nate smiled. He looked at Sarah and watched her take a sip of coffee and then looked at Amanda, who was pulling Mittens into her lap. He sure liked the two ladies a lot and felt a special connection to them after the strange events of this night. "Well," he said, finding a spot at the round kitchen table to sit down in, "I met my wife right here in Prate many years back. My wife was a fugitive from the law, you see."

"Really?" Amanda exclaimed.

Nate chuckled to himself. "Nah, just making sure you're paying attention is all."

Amanda made a silly face at Nate. "Don't make me pour my coffee down the back of your pants. I want the goods. Now start talking."

Nate winked at Sarah. "Well, my wife came into my life on a hot, dry day," Nate began. Sarah and Amanda snuggled up to his story, Nate's warm voice making them feel like two happy girls cuddling up against a soothing fire. "My truck went and had a flat, leaving me standing beside the road wondering whether to walk into town for a spare or walk back here to this here farm for a nice drink of cold water first. As I was debating with myself, a truck came driving down the road and stopped to see if I needed help."

"Oh, and the driver of the truck was your wife, right?" Amanda asked in a dreamy voice.

"Nope," Nate said and patted Amanda's hand, "just old Mason Buckles. Mason gave me a ride into town and dropped me off at Old Man Rider's garage," Nate explained and then paused. He tipped his ears toward the stove. "Beans will be needing water soon."

"Oh," Amanda pouted, "don't stop now. Keep talking, please."

"Well," Nate continued, "I bought myself a spare tire and started the long walk back to my truck and didn't get no farther than Whitfield Street before I saw a beautiful young woman sitting on the front lawn of a little white house, looking as bored as you could imagine. I walked up to her and said: 'Now, why are you sitting out here in this here heat looking the way you do? Don't you have enough sense to go inside where's it's cool?'"

"You didn't," Amanda gasped.

"I sure enough did," Nate said in a matter-of-fact voice. "My future wife was out baking in the sun, which told me she didn't have a lick of sense in her head."

"What did she say back to you?" Sarah asked.

"Oh, she gave me a sour face and told me to buzz off down the road," Nate answered Sarah. "My future wife wasn't a woman to be talked down to."

"Serves you right," Amanda told Nate. "So what if your wife was sitting out in the sun? Maybe she was just outside enjoying the day?"

"Nope," Nate corrected Amanda. "My future wife was outside baking in the sun because her folks were inside bickering up a storm and she didn't want to hear another word of it." Nate reached out and patted Mittens on the head. The puppy was getting sleepy and starting to drop its head in Amanda's lap. "My wife's daddy was a nasty drinker, you see, and a hard man to get along with, even when he wasn't hitting the bottle."

"Oh," Amanda said and shook her head. "I hate alcohol. My husband isn't allowed near a whiskey bottle."

"Smart woman," Nate told Amanda, "but my wife's mother wasn't so smart. That woman put up with a good amount of abuse before finally going to Heaven. She knew Jesus said you couldn't divorce your better half unless that person either died or cheated on you, so she remained faithful to her husband until the day she died."

"Old-timers were...special," Sarah sighed. "Today, people run to a divorce lawyer at the drop of a hat."

"Don't you know it, don't you know it...shame, shame," Nate grunted to himself. "Why my niece has been married three times and it don't look like her third husband is going to be sticking 'round much longer." Nate shook his head. "Three times...how can a woman get married three times? Don't make sense in my mind. Man and woman are supposed to marry for love and make that love last for life, not a few months."

"I know," Sarah sighed. The image of her husband floated

into her mind. "But it's complicated. People forget love is supposed to matter."

Amanda saw sadness enter her best friend's eyes. "Are you okay, love?"

"Sure," Sarah forced a weak smile to her face. "I don't have any other choice but to be okay."

Nate read Sarah's face. He saw hurt and anger, grief and pain, all mixed up into one vicious pill that wasn't going down easy. "Well," he said and continued on with his story, in hopes that his words would make Sarah feel better, "I didn't buzz off. Instead, I sat right down on the grass beside my wife and asked her what bee had crawled into her bonnet? My future wife tossed her thumb at the house behind her and that's when I heard an ugly commotion going on in the kitchen. I reckon it was then that I kicked myself in the backside, figuratively speaking, of course."

"I bet," Amanda said.

"I had done gone and acted a fool without understanding the situation," Nate reminisced. "My future wife was sitting out in the sun because her heart was breaking, not because she didn't have any sense to her." Nate bit down on her lip. "My, was she pretty sitting on the grass, though...prettiest woman I ever saw."

"What happened after you realized the truth?" Sarah asked.

"Oh, I sat silent for a few minutes and then asked my future wife if she wanted to take a walk with a dumb old rock," Nate answered Sarah and chuckled to himself. "I didn't have time to take no walk because I had chores to tend to, but I sure wanted to take a walk with her something fierce. And to my shock, instead of slugging me in the mouth, she agreed to take a walk with me. But only if I agreed to leave the spare tire in her yard and wash my hands first."

"Nate, Prate must have been even smaller back then," Sarah said. "You never saw your wife before?"

"Nope," Nate said. "Man can't see a woman who just moved to town."

"Oh, I see," Sarah replied.

"Yep, my wife and her folks were new in town and old Nate was the first man to say hello."

"Fate," Amanda sighed.

"A blessing," Nate smiled. "So anyway, me and my future wife took us a long walk down to Dove River and let our feet soak in the cold water for a bit. We talked some, about this or that, and then walked back to Whitfield Street. By this time my wife's daddy had wandered off someplace and her momma was in the kitchen cooking lunch. So I picked up my tire and said goodbye and walked on back to my truck...but I walked back the happiest man alive."

"That's it?" Amanda asked. "No first kiss in the rain...no holding hands...no valiant battle to win her hand?"

Nate smiled. "Three days later I went back and asked her to marry me," he told Amanda. "I reckon I was a bit crazy, and my wife sure thought so—and so did her folks—but I was bound and determined to marry the woman who completed the other side of my heart. I marched myself right up on her front porch, knocked on the door, and when her daddy answered I told him what my intentions were and waited to be shot. But glory be, ladies, the man was stone cold sober that day, and because he was in a hurry to marry off his daughter, agreed in no time at all."

"What did your wife have to say?" Sarah asked.

Nate chuckled. "My wife knew I'd be coming back and had her suitcase already packed. I took her to the preacher man that very day and home to this farm that very night. And from then on, we were inseparable...soul mates forever. Now, I'm not saying our marriage was easy. No ma'am. I spent many hours out in the fields working from dawn to dusk and my wife spent many hours learning how to be a wife to a man who tended to the land. We just...sorta had to figure each other out a little and work out the kinks...but in time, we fit together like a soft hand in a smooth glove."

"You met your future wife, insulted her, walked her down to some river, and then came back three days later and married her," Amanda said and shook her head. "I guess in those days things were different."

"Nah," Nate smiled at Amanda, "folks today, if they knew what love was? They wouldn't wait years to get married by a preacher man. No time for courting and fussing and all that. Back in the old days, when a man knew he loved a woman he didn't wait a second, he just came right out and told her. If the woman felt the same toward him, then they went and got married. If the woman didn't feel the same, the man moved on without whining to the wind."

"It took close to two years for my stubborn husband to propose to me," Amanda complained. "Mr. Nervous was the kind of bloke who didn't want to 'rush' our relationship. Why he made me wait for something I knew was going to eventually happen is beyond me."

Nate chuckled to himself again, stood up, and walked over to the kitchen sink. "I bet you would have slugged your husband if he made you wait another day."

"I would have," Amanda promised.

Nate filled up a green drinking glass full of hot water and added it to the pot of beans. "What about you, Sarah? How did you meet your husband?"

Sarah tensed up. "Oh, at a private party," she said and stumbled over her words. "I...a lady who

I...uh...saved...invited me to the party as a way of saying thank you."

"Saved?" Nate asked.

"Yes, I..." Sarah paused and shook her head. "A gunman entered a grocery store...I ducked for cover...I grabbed a lady who was in danger and pulled her down to the floor with me. Once she was safe, I grabbed my gun and managed to shoot the gunman...it wasn't anything, really. Any cop would have done the same."

"Yeah, but you were the cop on the scene," Nate told Sarah and nodded at her. "You're a good cop. And a mighty brave woman."

"So is Amanda," Sarah said and turned the attention to her best friend and began telling Nate about how brave and daring Amanda had been during their Alaska cases. "She saved my life more than once. I owe this woman my life."

Amanda blushed. Nate tilted his head at her. "Is this all true?" he asked. Amanda humbly nodded. "I never took you for a coward," he smiled at Amanda. "I figured you had a grizzly sleeping inside of you."

"Well, maybe I was a tad daring in my exploits," Amanda admitted, "but I was also very, very scared...and cold...blimey, was it ever cold."

"Freezing," Sarah emphasized. "And speaking of

freezing, that reminds me. My poor coffee shop is collecting dust right now. Amanda, when we get home, I have to dust off the coffee pots and open up shop for a few hours."

Amanda grinned and shook her head regretfully. "Sure, love," she said.

Sarah stared at Amanda. "What's that supposed to mean? Wait...I know. It's my coffee, isn't it? I make my coffee too strong."

"A tad," Amanda confessed and winked at Nate. "My friend here makes her coffee strong enough to put hair on the butt of a bald seal."

"Is that right?" Nate laughed and stirred the beans. "My wife sure made her coffee strong, too. Why, there were times that I went to work so wired up that I wasn't sure which way to turn."

Sarah smiled. "Seems like me and your wife have something in common."

Nate pointed at Amanda. "You and her both," he said. "You all three have good hearts resting in your souls. That's a rare find in today's world. Folks today, men and women, are too busy worrying about them little phones they carry around rather than getting married and raising a family. That niece of mine keeps her face stuck to her little phone tapping out these little messages and chatting with a hundred people at once...too busy being busy with her phone to understand her life is empty."

Sarah began to reply but before she could, someone knocked on the back door. Sarah jumped to her feet and snatched her gun up. Nate shook his head and put his finger to his mouth. Amanda pulled the puppy closer to her chest. Outside, the stranger knocked on the back door again.

"Who's knocking on my back door this time of night?" Nate called out.

"It's Harry, you old grouch," a voice fussed from the back porch. "It's our card night, remember?"

"Well I'll be," Nate said and shook his head. He apologized to the women. "Old Nate done went and forgot all about Uno night." Nate walked over to the back door, disengaged the lock, and pulled the door open. A man about Nate's age stepped into the kitchen, his wrinkled face dominated by a pair of grumpy eyes. "Come on in, Harry." Sarah quickly put her gun away and sat down.

Harry spotted Sarah sitting down and shot Nate an indignant eye. "You forgot me over a pair of pretty gals, huh?"

"No, no," Nate fussed back.

Sarah grinned. Harry was the spitting image of Nate,

clothes and all. Worn blue jeans, faded and patched flannel shirts with pearl buttons worn down by years of use, and carefully trimmed hair beneath a cap with a seed company logo above the brim. The only difference between Harry and Nate was that Harry was Asian, perhaps Chinese, but Sarah couldn't be certain. "Who are you?" Harry asked and tossed a deck of Uno cards down onto the kitchen table. "You the fuzz?"

"Oh, good grief, man," Nate griped, "will you sit down and close your mouth?" Nate closed the back door and locked it. "Harry Widster, this is Sarah, retired detective, and her friend Amanda, staying here for the night while...uh, while they get their car fixed. Beans will be done shortly. We'll all eat and play us some Uno until we're ready to take a gander at the back of our eyelids."

"Not me," Harry shook his head. "Insomnia isn't letting me sleep but three or four hours a night." Harry looked to Sarah and Amanda for sympathy. "I wish I could sleep."

"You can sleep, you old coot," Nate complained. "And you would, too, if you'd stop drinking a pot of coffee before bed."

Harry waved a hand at Nate in irritation. "Coffee has nothing to do with it. Dr. Dalton said—"

"Dr. Dalton will say anything to keep paranoid old farts like you dishing out money for useless office visits," Nate exclaimed and walked back to the stove, mumbling to himself.

Sarah and Amanda both grinned at each other. "I've got insomnia," Harry insisted and threw his hand at Nate. "That old man doesn't know what he's talking about."

"At least I don't cheat at Uno," Nate commented as he stirred the beans.

"Are you saying that I do?" Harry shot back.

"I don't chew my cabbage twice, old man," Nate replied and shook the wooden spoon in his hand at Harry. "You know it ain't right to hold them draw four cards till the end."

"Says who?" Harry argued. "The rules doesn't say I can't hold my draw four cards. You're just a poor loser."

"I'll poor loser you," Nate said and gritted his teeth. "Must be out of my mind to play Uno with a cheat like you—"

"Uh, how long have you two known each other?" Sarah asked, hoping to de-escalate the argument.

"Since we were knee-high to a toad frog," Nate replied, the sourness fading.

"I was the best man at Nate's wedding," Harry said in a proud voice.

"You sure were," Nate smiled. And just like that, the

argument was over and the warmth of friendship began to glow. "Old Harry and me go way back. His momma dropped him off at the orphanage that used to be in these parts and made tracks." Nate shook his head. "Skinniest kid I ever saw. Shameful."

Harry folded his arms together. "The orphanage got me work on Nate's farm when his daddy was working the land. I'd come out here and work with Nate and his daddy five days a week."

"Yes sir," Nate said, "Harry was sure a good worker. My daddy sure loved him, too, and so did my momma."

"It wasn't long before they adopted me," Harry said in a proud tone. "I kept my ma's name. But Nate and me became brothers."

"That's right," Nate smiled at Harry in a way only an old friend could. "Me and Harry are tighter than ticks."

Harry beamed. "Nate's daddy helped me buy my own farm. I was sure happy about that because I didn't want to leave Prate, but I knew someday I would have to make a life for myself."

"Uh huh," Nate continued for Harry. "Harry's farm is just a stretch down the road. He did real well for himself, too. Ended up selling farm equipment along with his crops. Smart man."

"Are you married?" Amanda asked Harry.

"My Julia went to be with Jesus five years ago," Harry told Amanda and grew silent.

"I'm sorry, I didn't mean to—"

Harry lifted his right hand. "Don't be sorry," he said in a soft voice. "My Julia is waiting for me just like Nate's wife is waiting for him."

"Two fine women waiting for us," Nate said.

"The best," Harry agreed. He looked at Sarah. "Is that your dog?"

"It belongs to my best friend Amanda here. The puppy is Mittens," Sarah said.

Harry focused on Amanda. "Are you from England?"

"Why, yes," Amanda smiled. "But I live in Alaska with my husband now. A little town called Snow Falls. Sarah lives there, too. We're on our way to Los Angeles but we had a flat tire and Nate picked us up."

Nate carefully turned around and met Sarah's eyes—she nodded, knowing what he was asking—then he turned back and began stirring the beans again. "Harry, these two women are in some kind of trouble," he said. "After I picked them up off the road, some gun-happy lunatic driving one of them fancy cars came racing at us with guns blazing." Nate turned around and pointed the wooden spoon he was holding at Sarah. "She is a retired homicide detective from Los Angeles. The Sheriff reckons that has something to do with it."

"A detective?" Harry asked.

"Retired," Sarah stated.

"A cop never retires," Harry corrected Sarah.

Nate studied Sarah's face and then continued. "Somebody went and killed a woman she knows and dumped the body in her jeep while we were down at Monroe's farm. Sheriff Bufford is as mad as a wet hornet, too. He's forcing her to stay in town and solve the murder herself. He's deputizing her in the morning."

"Do you expect anything more from Paul?" Harry asked with a chuckle. "The only thing that man knows about the law is how to spell the word."

Amanda fought back laughter. Sarah bit down on her bottom lip. "Sheriff Bufford seems...a bit overwhelmed," Amanda managed to say.

"Overwhelmed my foot," Harry cackled. "Paul Bufford has the IQ of swamp gas and everyone knows it."

"Don't matter how smart Paul is or isn't," Nate pointed out, "because we were shot at and a woman was killed."

The mention of the murder of Rebecca sobered Sarah's mind. Rebecca's death tugged at her heart. Even though they had not been close, she had cherished their connection and she knew she would have to put those feelings away in order to focus on the case. It made her sick to think that Rebecca might have been killed as part of a plot to warn her away from Los Angeles. The antics between Nate and Harry had been amusing, but it was time to focus back on the case at hand. "The people who killed Rebecca could still be around," she said in a cautious voice. "Harry, you didn't pass anybody on the road on your way over here, did you?"

"A couple of bored deer was all my old eyes saw," Harry informed Sarah. "I guess we're not playing Uno tonight, Nate."

"Why not?" Nate asked. "Ain't no sense in sitting here worrying ourselves sick over something we can't change."

"True," Harry agreed. "Beans ready?"

"Get the bowls and I'll cut the cornbread."

Sarah watched Nate and Harry prepare their late dinner with her tired eyes drooping. The puppy had eaten and curled up on a cushion in the corner and fallen asleep. When Nate brought Sarah a bowl of pinto beans and cornbread, she gave him a grateful smile even though she was no longer hungry. "Looks good."

"Want a slice of onion?" Harry asked.

"No thanks," Sarah said. She looked at Amanda. "Onion?"

"Sure, why not," Amanda replied and winked at Nate. "We'll have onion breath together."

"Beans ain't fit without a slice of onion," Nate agreed.

After Harry and Nate brought the food to the table, Nate poured four glasses of cold iced tea and sat down. "Lord, we thank you from our hearts for this food because You feed Your children. In Jesus' sweet name, amen."

"Amen," Amanda smiled and grabbed her spoon. "I'm starved. Let's eat."

Sarah picked up her spoon and slowly took a bite of beans. "We're going to see what we can dig up, first thing in the morning," she told Nate and glanced at Amanda. "Amanda is my partner. She'll help me get to the core of this case."

"You're dealing with mighty dangerous people," Nate warned Sarah. "This here is Prate, not Los Angeles. It's easier to kill someone in the woods and not be seen than on a crowded sidewalk in front of a bunch of watchful eyes."

"You think the people who killed Rebecca might try and kill me?" Sarah asked.

"Maybe the rats who are after you killed that woman as a way to warn you off," Nate said in a thoughtful voice and took a bite of cornbread, "and maybe they left town? But then again, maybe not."

"Maybe they're hanging back to see if I'll take their message seriously," Sarah said.

Nate nodded. "Yep. Don't make sense for the bad guys to go through so much trouble and then go back to where they came from without being sure their message was taken seriously."

Amanda took a hearty bite of beans, savored their rich flavor after such a long, hungry day, and then grabbed her glass of tea. "Rebecca must have known the truth," she pointed out.

Sarah took a sip of her tea. "When I spoke to Rebecca this morning she seemed like her old self. Of course, she could have been acting. Rebecca did act in a few movies in her younger years." Sarah mused over this idea. "She seemed excited about the book deal with J&P Brothers...what changed between the time I called her and the time she was killed? Where was she when I called her? I need to find out her location."

"How?" Amanda asked. "Can you trace her cell phone somehow?"

"I'm not sure yet," Sarah confessed. "What I do know, and what I want everyone sitting at this table to know, is that Rebecca was a brilliant businesswoman. Her mind was sharper than the edge of a razor and her mouth was just as sharp when it came to dealing with those suits in Los Angeles. There's no way she would have walked into a trap. She's dead because she became a threat."

Harry's eyes widened to hear talk like this. Nate took a bite of beans followed by some onion and smiled at his friend, as if to indicate that things were still normal. "Let's back up a few steps," Nate told Sarah. "You were on the right track about wondering where that woman was at when you called her. That's a mighty important fact."

"I know," Sarah admitted. "I doubt she was in Prate, but she couldn't have been in Los Angeles, either. Where was she?"

"Love," Amanda said, as a sudden thought struck her, "when I asked how anyone could have known our location, you suggested that maybe your cell phone was being tracked. If that's true...uh, well, doesn't that mean the bad guys know where we're at right now?"

Nate glanced at the back door with calm eyes. "I guess we'll find out if bullets come flying through the kitchen at us," he said and took an unhurried bite.

Sarah pulled a piece of cornbread off. "I threw my cell phone out of the back of Nate's truck on the ride here," she told them. "The only place anyone is going to find my cell phone is in the woods."

"Oh, you're a darling," Amanda beamed.

Nate nodded. "Smart woman." Even Harry looked impressed.

Sarah lowered her eyes to the bowl of beans sitting before her. "I can't believe Rebecca got caught up in all this," she sighed. "Rebecca is dead...and it's my fault. If I had been smarter I would have asked her more questions. Instead, I acted like a giddy school girl. I should have known something was wrong."

"How?" Amanda asked. "Love, Rebecca called to inform you that a major studio wanted to turn your books into movies. You couldn't know it was a trap. That kind of news would have thrilled anyone to the bone. Why, if I had been you I would have done front flips all the way to Los Angeles. You can't blame yourself, love. You're only human."

"I'm also a cop," Sarah replied and raised her eyes. She wanted to condemn herself, but the truth was Amanda was right. How could she have known a trap was being set for her? "And as a cop, I need to start asking myself questions. Question one: where was Rebecca when I called her this morning? Question two: Why did they kill Rebecca and not me? Why did the people behind the killing give me a warning instead of killing me?"

"Time will tell," Amanda said and winced. "Yes, love, I'm afraid time is going to answer all of our questions in a very bad way." Amanda patted Mittens softly on her head. "It's always that way, you know...the answers you're seeking are given in bad ways. But me and you, Los Angeles, we're ready for the worst because we've dealt with the worst. So...well...bring it on, bad guys, right?"

Sarah looked at Nate and then at Harry and finally back to Amanda. She felt tired, angry, upset and scared. But what she felt most was the need to find answers. Someone didn't want her to take this trip to Los Angeles or sign this contract. Or worse, she thought without voicing her thoughts: someone was playing a very deadly game of cat and mouse that didn't even involve Rebecca, or anyone at J&P Brothers. It could be a deadly and intelligent killer out for revenge. For all she knew, the studio contract could have been a smokescreen to hide something much more nefarious. "I need to make a phone call," she said and looked at Harry with hopeful eyes. "Harry, please tell me you have a landline phone in your home."

Harry took a large bite of beans and chased them with a generous chug of tea. "I have a phone," he said and took another bite.

"Since when?" Nate asked.

"If you ever came over to my house instead of making me come here you would have seen that I had a phone installed in my house last year. I had to get rid of that awful cell phone my daughter sent me," Harry said grumpily. "I guess this means no Uno game after all," he grumbled.

"Harry please, I need to use your phone," Sarah pleaded.

Nate raised his right hand. "Calm down," he urged Sarah. "Let's fill our bellies and let our brains settle a while and then we'll take a drive over to Harry's."

"I'll have seconds if you don't mind," Amanda told Nate and lifted her bowl in the air. "I'll also have some more cornbread. No sense in dying hungry."

Sarah drew in a deep breath and decided Amanda was right. What was the sense in being hungry? she thought. It was going to be a long night. "I think I'll have seconds, too," she told Nate and finished her beans so she could pass him her empty bowl. Outside in the dark night, shreds of clouds roamed past the moon with twisted faces.

arry's home was nearly identical to Nate's, except Harry's home seemed to be stuck in the 1950s instead of the 1930s. Like Nate's home, Harry's place was clean, warm and welcoming. "Phone is hanging next to the refrigerator. I had it put there because it's easy to remember," Harry told Sarah in a self-important voice. "My hearing aid made me think that ugly cell phone was ringing from every room in the house. Now I know when I hear a phone ring to make a path into the kitchen. Just like in the old days when everybody had a landline."

"You need to get a phone," Amanda told Nate and drew in a deep breath of cinnamon. Harry's kitchen was delightful.

"Nope," Nate replied in a stubborn voice. "I ain't never had a phone and never intend to. Ain't right for folks to be so lazy when they want to talk to each other. Folks need to visit one another and say hello in person. Neighbors need to sit and talk to each other."

"That old fart," Harry told Amanda. "My brother's set in his ways. Trying to convince him to get a phone would be like trying to convince a pebble to turn into a marshmallow."

"You're the one to talk. You swore you'd never get a phone. You sure didn't keep your word," Nate fired back at Harry.

"My daughter told me to get a phone or she was going to hire a live-in caretaker," Harry told Nate. "You know we ain't those kind of people, Nate."

Nate shoved his hands down into the pockets of his pants. "Why didn't you say so in the first place? I would have understood."

"You've been worrying over your cancer and—" Harry stopped talking. His face became sorrowful. "Nate, I'm sorry. It was a slip of the tongue."

"No worries," Nate promised his friend with a gentle smile.

"You have cancer?" Amanda asked Nate with a broken heart.

"Prostate," Nate fumbled for the right words, "illness

comes with age. But don't you worry, Old Nate still has some good years left."

Sarah looked into Nate's eyes. The old man was ready to die and go home to Jesus but he was also willing to wait out his time in good spirit. "Nate, if there is anything we can do—"

Nate shook his head. "Nothing for me. Now, you better make your call."

Sarah understood Nate's reply and made her call. "Pete...yeah, it's Sarah. I—"

"Finally decided to call me," Pete griped as he maneuvered his sturdy old Honda Accord through the back roads of Northern California.

"I had to get rid of my cell phone. And I haven't been able to get to a phone until just now, Pete. I'm sorry," Sarah said. "I'm really far out in the country here."

"Yeah, yeah," Pete continued to drive, his knuckles white as he gripped the wheel. He snatched up a water bottle and took a drink of cold water. "The sheriff up there gave me a call, kid. I heard about the body, so I decided to come your way and make an appearance. When you wouldn't answer your cell phone, I got even more worried."

"I'm sorry. Sheriff Bufford told me you were coming," Sarah told Pete in a grateful voice. "Pete, I want to see you, but not like this...I hoped it would be under better circumstances. That said, I'm sure glad you're coming."

"Me, too, kid," Pete told Sarah in a nostalgic voice. "Looks like you are I are going to be working together again, just like old times."

"Yeah," Sarah said in a worried tone. "Pete, there's something wrong," she said and glanced over her shoulder at Amanda, Nate, and Harry.

"Bufford gave me the description of the body. Sounds like your book agent ended up dead in your jeep," Pete said and took another drink of water. "Yeah, kid, I'd say something is wrong." Pete focused his eyes on the road. He hated driving at night, but when duty called, he responded. His old partner was in danger and he wasn't about to sit by and wait for the sun to rise before hitting the trail. "Talk to me, partner. Tell me everything from the beginning."

Hearing Pete call her "partner" thrilled Sarah and broke her heart at the same time. Suddenly she felt the stirrings of all her memories from when she was a homicide detective living back in Los Angeles. The cases she had tackled in Alaska were risky and dangerous, but each case had an Alaskan character to them—in a snowy environment that was far away from the hot city streets of Los Angeles. Being outside the bounds of Alaska and caught up in a murder case with Pete at her side again felt oddly natural. It stirred something in her. She swallowed and tried to ignore the butterflies. "It's like this Pete," Sarah said. "It all started when Rebecca called my cabin in Alaska last week..."

Sarah's tone worried Amanda. She noticed her best friend had said 'in Alaska' instead of 'at home.' She sighed and looked down at her hands. "Stay with me, girl," she whispered. Meanwhile, Sarah had finished giving Pete the details of what they knew so far.

"Okay, this is bigger than I thought. I'll check J&P Brothers out and shake them down for information," Pete told Sarah. He slowed down a little, thinking through their strategy. "In the meantime, get yourself to Los Angeles where you belong. Forget about running this case from farm country. Our HQ is my office," Pete ordered Sarah. "I'm turning my car around and making tracks for the bright lights of Los Angeles. If the killer took the trouble to kill Rebecca and trace you all the way to Prate, they are certainly still in Prate, just waiting for you to make a false move. You've got to get out of there for your safety, investigation or no investigation."

Sarah bit down on her lip. She knew Pete was right. But Sheriff Bufford was going to be spitting mad in the morning if she didn't show up to be deputized. Still, Sarah thought, if a killer was playing a sick game with her, it would be better to stand on a level playing field instead of remaining out in the middle of nowhere. "Okay, partner. Amanda and I will leave at first light."

"If Sheriff Bufford tries to stop you, tell him to give me a call," Pete told Sarah and spotted an all-night gas station glowing in the dark. He sped into the parking lot, turned sharply to pull back out in the other direction, and raced back toward Los Angeles. "Okay kid, I'm driving back south."

"I'll be on the road just as soon as I get a tire for my jeep," Sarah promised, "I'll be right on your tail."

"Good," Pete said and snatched a cigar out of the car's ashtray and shoved it into the corner of his mouth. "I'll be checking on the studio until you plant your backside in my office."

"Also check on a woman named Mrs. Diane Samton. This woman supposedly works for J&P Brothers, Pete. It's the only name I have to go on right now. And—"

"Sniff through the dead woman's office," Pete said, "yeah, yeah, kid, I know, I know. I already sent people over to her office."

"Check her—"

"Phone records. Yeah, Yeah," Pete said. "I'm not a wet-behind-the-ears rookie, kid."

"I know, Pete," Sarah replied. "She's not just some dead woman to me, Pete. Rebecca was a close friend, not just my agent," she explained. "She deserves the absolute best from us."

"Yep," Pete agreed, "and she's going to get the absolute best. From this point on, you're a homicide detective again. I'll pass the paperwork through the department and get you back on course."

Sarah felt excitement and fear grip her. "Hey, Pete, I...I don't know. I'm retired."

"You just took some time off to go play with some polar bears," Pete barked. "Now get your butt back home and get back to work Detective Garland!" Pete yelled. "Stay safe, Sarah," he said in a softer voice, and ended the call abruptly.

"Love?" Amanda asked.

Sarah hung up the phone and turned to face Amanda. "June Bug," she said, "we need to tackle this case from Los Angeles. We're in a strange town with very few resources at our disposal. We don't know this area of the country, the roads, the people or the history. We're vulnerable right now in more ways than one."

Amanda understood Sarah's concerns. "You're the boss," she said and forced a sad smile to her face. "It does seem like the killer wants you to stay away from Los Angeles, so maybe our answers are waiting for us there."

Sarah nodded. "Even if we don't find any answers, at least we'll be on my turf."

"Ain't no such thing," Nate warned Sarah. "Never forget

that a person set on harming you can do so anywhere. People who lock their windows and doors become victims in their own homes."

"If we stay here, Nate, we're vulnerable," Sarah pointed out. "I have a dead friend, an unknown killer on the loose, a lazy sheriff insisting I do his job, and a lot of unanswered questions and sharp edges to get around. On top of all of that, I have a plate full of uncertainties that I have to digest. I need to be in a familiar place around faces I know and trust."

"I'm someone you know and trust," Amanda told Sarah. "We're a team, remember?"

"Of course we are," Sarah assured Amanda and walked over to her. "We'll always be a team, June Bug. And as a team, our best option is to meet up with Pete in Los Angeles."

Amanda looked deeply into Sarah's eyes. She saw urgency and determination burning in a heart that was prepared to fight an unknown enemy. "Okay," she said and nodded, "we'll meet your friend in Los Angeles if you think that's best." Amanda looked at Nate. For some reason—a reason she couldn't explain to herself—she didn't want to leave Nate.

Sarah followed Amanda's eyes with her own. She saw Nate staring at her with eyes that looked straight into her heart. Nate was reading her like a book. "You can fight from here," he told her with a pleading look.

"Why?" Sarah asked. "It would be foolish to stay here, Nate. I'm out of my territory in Prate. I don't know anyone and can't depend on the local law enforcement guys. I don't know my way around and—"

"You have a lot of excuses," Nate barked at Sarah. "I thought you were smart."

"Sarah is smart," Amanda promised Nate. "She outwitted a very dangerous woman who killed her adoptive father without any sweat at all. Sarah is a firecracker in a pot of oatmeal when it comes to solving murder cases."

"Maybe so," Nate said, keeping his eyes locked on Sarah, "but her brain ain't working too smart right now."

"What do you mean by that?" Sarah insisted.

"Your lady friend ended up dead in your jeep and you have no idea why, but all of sudden you're ready to up and leave the crime scene without any answers."

"I don't think I'm going to find any answers here in Prate. The sheriff said he found Rebecca's purse in my jeep," Sarah explained.

"Yep," Nate said.

"Nate, Rebecca's body was a message left by the killer.

The killer can hardly be someone from around here, meaning it wouldn't be useful to stick around and question the locals. I doubt the autopsy report is going to show anything useful and besides, I don't need to be in Prate to receive the report. I can call from Los Angeles—"

"You said the killer might be warning you to stay away from Los Angeles," Nate interrupted. "What if the killer is trying to lure you to Los Angeles? Say someone who knows you well enough to bet that you won't back down from this fight? Did your brain ever consider that?"

Sarah grew silent. Her mind was considering many different options. Was the killer somehow connected to the studio? Was the killer an old enemy setting a game for her to play? Was the killer someone who wanted Rebecca dead and wanted to pin the murder on her? Sarah didn't know. All she knew was that the J&P Brothers deal was likely a ploy to lure her back to Los Angeles. Or, so it seemed. But the death of Rebecca and her body being dumped in her jeep that was broken down on the side of a long, rural road in the middle of nowhere made Sarah begin asking many frustrating questions: how did the killer know her location? Where was Rebecca when she called her earlier in the morning? Why did the killer make himself known conducting an obvious attack on the road? Who was the killer? Why was she being targeted? "Maybe you're right, Nate. Maybe the killer set a challenge for me to answer or maybe Rebecca's death was a warning to stay away from Los Angeles."

"I thought that in the beginning," Nate told Sarah, "and even believed it. But then I began thinking about that fancy BMW. Now, the driver of that fancy car was shooting at us, but there's not a single bullet hole in my truck. I checked."

"So did I," Sarah added.

"Seems mighty strange to me that there ain't a single bullet hole," Nate continued. "It's almost like the killer was toying with us...like he was just having a bit of fun for now. But," Nate pointed out, "if I had found bullet holes in my truck, then maybe I would believe the killer was warning you to stay away from Los Angeles."

"So what you're saying is that because you didn't find any bullet holes..." Amanda rubbed her chin, "that means the killer was sending a message to Sarah that...he was playing some kind of sick game?"

"Yep," Nate gave her a thumbs-up.

Sarah stared into Nate's eyes. "Like a dare?" she asked, testing it out in her mind.

"Maybe, who knows?" Nate replied. "Either way, the killer wanted you to know he's in control and wants you to run back to the only place you feel in control. My suggestion is to stay around Prate and do Paul's job for him and force the killer to show himself."

Sarah felt a cold chill walk down her spine. Nate was

speaking the truth. Los Angeles could be a death trap and she could be playing right into the killer's hands. "Okay, Nate, I'll stick around for a few days," she promised and focused on Amanda. She saw relief explode in her best friend's eyes. "You didn't want to work on the investigation from Los Angeles, did you?"

"Not after Rebecca's death," Amanda confessed. "Love, I trust you and I'll follow you to the big city, but I agree with Nate. I think we need to stay right here and try to draw the killer out into the open."

"Smart move," Harry jumped into the conversation with both feet. "Lead a fly to honey, don't taunt a bear with vinegar."

"I guess I better call Pete," Sarah said and walked back to the phone. Oh Pete, she thought to herself, I miss you so much...but I am a cop and my gut is telling me to stay out of Los Angeles even though my heart wants to go home. And there's no bullet holes in Nate's truck, not a single one.

The following morning, Nate drove Sarah and Amanda into the small town of Prate. "This looks like Mayberry from that old show, you know, The Andy Griffith Show?" Amanda looked to her left at the old buildings lining Main Street. "Look at that," she exclaimed and pointed to an old two-story courthouse at the end of the street on a small but well-manicured lot. "We're in Mayberry."

Nate chuckled to himself. His belly was full of pancakes, eggs and coffee and his mind was rested enough to face another day. "I think Mayberry was a tad bigger."

Sarah glanced to her right and saw an old hardware store with three run-down trucks parked out front. "What do you think, girl?" she asked Mittens, who was perched in her lap and happily watching out the window. "Could you live in a town like this?" Mittens looked up at Sarah and tilted her head as if considering the question. When Sarah looked out the window again, she spotted an old woman and old man venturing into a thrift shop next to the hardware store. The town felt depressingly empty. Despite its beautiful old courthouse and scenic views, it was a dying town, its few residents just scuttling along in what was left. With all the dark and empty storefronts, Sarah had the feeling that a dark shadow was peering out at them, lurking, watching and waiting. The puppy whined uneasily and looked at Sarah for reassurance. "I didn't think so," Sarah said, ruffling the puppy's ears to soothe her.

"Sheriff's office is in the basement of the courthouse," Nate said and stopped at a stop sign. He pointed to his left. "That way leads to the grocery store, garage, and some more little businesses." Nate pointed to his right. "That way leads out of town and into some residential neighborhoods, like the ones we passed driving in." Nate tossed a thumb over his shoulder. "And of course, that way leads back home."

Sarah looked to her left and right. The city of Prate was stretched out like a giant T with a circle around it. "Easy enough," she said and focused her attention on the courthouse. The courthouse resembled a large log cabin rather than a typical community building. She spotted Sheriff Bufford standing in the parking lot to the left of the courthouse. "Okay Nate, drive us to the courthouse."

Nate eased through the stop sign, pulled into the parking lot and parked his truck next to Sheriff Bufford's car. "Nice morning, huh, Paul?"

Paul glanced up. The sky was warm and blue. "No," he said testily, and pointed at Sarah. "I received a very unpleasant call last night," he barked. "It seems your friend Pete isn't happy you're staying in Prate and ordered me to run you out of town."

"Oh, Pete," Sarah moaned.

Paul marched around to the passenger side door and pointed a finger at Sarah. "I don't take kindly to city folk calling me and ordering me around at all hours of the night. I have half a mind to agree with your friend. I'll manage the investigation somehow. Anyway, I'd have a heap less trouble without you outsiders mucking around in town and stirring up trouble."

"No," Sarah said and shook her head.

"No?" Paul asked and gave Sarah a hard look. "What makes you think it's your decision?"

"This is America, Sheriff. I'm free to stay anywhere I choose within the boundaries of the law. I haven't broken any laws, which means I can remain in Prate for as long as I like. Now, unless you'd like to lock me up and have my face and yours smeared across every local paper in the vicinity, and this story on the lips of every local gossip, you better reconsider."

Paul gritted his teeth. "I was...wrong to ask for your help. You can stay...but not as a badge, do you understand? And keep your gun secure and mind your p's and q's, or I'll find a reason to bring you in, gossip or no gossip!" Paul yelled and stormed away into the courthouse.

"Fussy little guss, isn't he?" Amanda asked in a disgusted voice. All she wanted to do was locate her luggage and change into a fresh dress. But unfortunately, Sarah had insisted on visiting the courthouse before venturing to the garage to retrieve her jeep. "Love, why did you want to come to the courthouse first?" she asked. "We need fresh clothes and I will die if I cannot get to my deodorant."

Sarah opened the passenger side door and stepped out. "If I'm being watched," she said, "I want them to think I'm not leaving Prate. And I think I am being watched." Sarah carefully glanced around as she set Mittens down

87

on the sidewalk. "Go use the bathroom, girl." Mittens walked over to Paul's car and squatted down next to his rear tire. Amanda watched from inside the truck's cab and stifled a giggle at the puppy's choice. "Good girl." As Mittens relieved herself, Sarah continued to walk her eyes around. Nate saw her looking and followed her gaze, too. She searched the courthouse, the open field behind the courthouse, and then allowed her eyes to stroll back down Main Street. And there, all of a sudden, the gray BMW shot out of an alley, raced toward the courthouse, hung a left, and sped away.

"Get in!" Nate called out to Sarah, readying himself.

"You're not going to catch that car, Nate," Sarah said as she watched the BMW vanish from her sight.

"I know that," Nate said, "but it ain't going to do us no good just sitting here, either. We might be able to spot him somewhere down the road."

"No. He wants us to follow him," Sarah told Nate. "Come on, let's go in the courthouse."

Nate looked down the street and figured Sarah was right. He climbed out of the truck and helped Amanda plant her feet on solid ground. "Thank you, sir," Amanda said in a worried voice. She turned to Sarah and motioned around town with her right hand. "How did the killer know we would be here of all places, love?"

"Exactly," Sarah said and bit down on her lower lip as

frustration gripped her heart. She looked directly at the courthouse. "Only person I called this morning was the sheriff."

Nate rubbed the back of his neck. "Now wait a minute, Paul might be a stiff piece of wood, but he's an honest man."

Sarah heard the sound of screeching tires and craned her neck to the left. She spotted the BMW speeding down the road, preparing to make a second run past the courthouse. "Get down," she yelled to her companions, dropped down to one knee, yanked out her gun, and began firing at the BMW. Two bullets hit the front windshield of the BMW and it skidded, nearly causing it to smash into a parked truck as the glass spidered into cracks, but the driver regained control at the last second and sped off down a residential street.

"Not bad," Nate congratulated Sarah as he stood up.

"This doesn't make any sense," Amanda huffed in an angry voice. "Why would they dare make a second pass at us? What kind of game is he playing?"

"The driver of that car was trying to force us to chase him," Sarah pointed out. "He was determined. But he won't be back anytime soon, though and—" Sarah heard Paul burst out of the courthouse and race toward them with his gun drawn. His face held a look of fury.

"What in tarnation—firing your gun in a public

environment—what do you—" Paul hollered, sputtering. "Explain yourself or I will arrest you and you will hand over your gun to me."

"If you try and take my gun I'll draw on you," Sarah promised Paul in a voice that forced Paul to back down. "I was defending myself. The gray BMW is back, Sheriff, and I managed to put two bullets in the front windshield. You need to get some patrols out right now and begin searching for that car."

"No," Paul objected. "I'm not sending panic through my town."

Sarah stared into Paul's eyes. "Last night you were very determined to make me do your job for you. Now, all of sudden, Sheriff, you want me to clear town."

"You're...bad news," Paul hissed at Sarah. "You and your friend brought a dark cloud into this town."

Nate saw fear in Paul's eyes—no, not fear, but downright terror. "What's eating at you, Paul? I ain't ever seen you act so hateful before. What's this woman done to you? She ain't no killer. She's one of the good people in this world."

Paul threw a hard eye at Nate. "You stay out of this, Nate. Go on back to your farm and stay there."

Sarah folded her arms. "Sheriff, if I didn't know better, I'd say the killer had a very serious talk with you."

Sarah's words seemed to punch Paul square in the face. The old man stepped away from her as if she were a contagious disease. "What? You're...crazy," he stuttered like a schoolyard kid searching for an intelligent response but only able to find a weak insult instead.

"Is she?" Amanda asked. "I know I'm not a seasoned detective, but I do know that BMW racing by here couldn't be a coincidence." Amanda stepped close to Paul. "Sarah called you this morning when we were having breakfast at Nate's and told you we were coming to the courthouse. You were the only one who knew we were on our way here."

Paul's anger and fear slowly began to transform into panic. "Listen to me," he tried to yell at Amanda, "if you're implying that I—"

"We are not implying. We are stating it. Perhaps you told the killer we would be arriving at this courthouse this morning," Sarah told Paul. "And perhaps a jury of your peers would be inclined to believe the same."

"A jury of my peers...wait a minute...I," Paul stuttered again, "I'm the sheriff, for crying out loud."

"You're not above the law," Sarah snapped. "Sheriff, I'm going to catch the killer and when I do, he's going to tell me everyone he's been in contact with. Everyone." She looked him in the eye without wavering. "Right now, this guy is running loose and trying to get everyone to run scared. I don't run from threats. Is that clear?"

Paul stared into Sarah's eyes and swallowed. Sarah's eyes were fierce and determined. "I..." he began and looked around, nervously. Sarah wondered suddenly if he was stalling for time, expecting to see the gray BMW appear again. Finally the sheriff seemed to collapse a little bit, his shoulders sagging. "I...he threatened my wife!"

Sarah folded her arms. "Who threatened your wife?" she demanded.

"I don't know the man's name," Paul confessed, feeling sweat begin to pour down his panicked face.

"Describe the man, then," Nate told Paul. "And calm your britches, too. Ain't no one standing here out to cause you no harm. If you were threatened the way you said you were, we sure ain't gonna stand here and condemn you for acting out of fear."

Paul threw a grateful look at Nate. "Nate, when I left George's place last night, I drove home. When I turned down the driveway, I saw a gray BMW sitting there, parked next to my wife's car. A man was leaning against the BMW...I knew he was bad news. But what could I do? I just couldn't run. My wife was inside the house for crying out loud. I thought I could talk him down or get him to leave or...something."

"I understand," Nate assured Paul.

Paul ran his sweaty hands over the front of his shirt. "I parked and got out of my car. The man...he didn't move an inch. He just waited for me to walk over to him and..." Paul paused as fear gripped his chest.

"And what?" Sarah pushed Paul.

Paul closed his eyes. "When he spoke...his voice was low and flat and calm, but he twisted it like the sharpest knife. He said he was here to chase you out of town, Sarah..." Paul shook his head. "And I was going to help him do it. But first, I was ordered to give you a message."

"What message?" Sarah asked, her adrenaline spiking.

He squeezed his eyes shut as if still in terror. "The man told me to tell you that Rebecca was just the first. She was just a warning. I was to tell you to...go back to Los Angeles and wait or more people are going to die," Paul answered Sarah and opened his eyes. He looked at her, pleadingly. "Beginning with my wife."

Sarah stared at Paul. So Rebecca's death wasn't a distraction intended to keep her away, she thought to herself, it was a warning to go to Los Angeles, at all costs. "I see," she said as her mind wandered around a confusing thought. "If the killer wanted me in Los Angeles, why didn't he just wait until I arrived?"

"How should I know?" Paul asked and raised a shaky hand at Sarah. "Detective Garland, the man who spoke to me last night called my home this morning. He gave me a number to call, and said he was watching the house. He knew exactly what my wife was wearing, it was as if he was watching us, but I couldn't see anyone outside. He ordered me to inform him of your movements as soon as I knew...about half an hour later you called me and told me you were driving to the courthouse with Nate. I...had no choice, can't you see that."

"I understand," Sarah assured Paul and placed a calm hand on his shoulder. "Sheriff, you contacted the killer, which means we can call him again at the same number, right?"

"What? Oh no," Paul objected and backed away from Sarah. "That man...that evil man...he will kill my wife if I dare go against him."

"Paul," Nate raised his hand into the air, "calm down, okay? Let's back up. Tell us what this man looked like. Describe him for us, okay?"

Paul wiped his arm across his mouth. "I..." he hesitated and looked around again. "The man was about average height...a little thick around the waist maybe...he had on...a leather jacket...blue jeans...and a baseball cap and sun glasses. It was dark and the man was obviously hiding his face."

Sarah let her mind soak in the new information and twist it around some. "About how old would you say the man was?" she finally asked.

Paul cast his eyes down at his wrinkled hands. "That's what scared me the most...I say man...but from his voice he couldn't have been more than twenty years old, maybe mid-twenties at the most."

"Really?" Amanda asked.

"A young voice despite all the evil he threatened," Paul promised. "Now listen, Detective, I...I'm sorry I played ball on the wrong team, but I have my wife to think about. You can try and arrest me, but I have plenty of people who will stand by me, too. So—"

"I have no intention of throwing the law in your face," Sarah assured Paul. "You and your wife were threatened. No one is going to blame you for trying to protect your wife." Sarah offered Paul a gentle smile. "Sheriff, I need the contact number the killer gave you. Please."

Paul swallowed again. "I—"

"You've already spilled the beans," Amanda spoke up. "The killer who paid you a visit isn't going to take you back. In for a penny, in for a pound, as they say. From this point forward, Sheriff, your only chance is to get on our team and play smart."

"She is speaking the truth," Nate told Paul. "Whoever this psycho kid is, he's obviously very deadly, Paul, and he ain't driving away from Prate singing sunshine songs, either. Sarah done went and shot out the windshield to that fancy car he's driving, which tells me that young man is as mad as a wet hornet right about now."

Paul looked around the little town and then focused on Sarah's eyes. "Detective Garland, the life of my wife and the safety of the people of this town are now in your hands," he said and pointed at the courthouse. "Come on, let's go talk in my office. I don't like standing out here in the open like this."

Sarah looked at Amanda and Nate. "Come on, guys," she said, "we stay together as a team."

"A team?" Nate asked.

Sarah nodded. "Nate, you're on our team for good," she smiled.

"Sure enough," Nate said, feeling useful again after many years of feeling like a worn-down firecracker. He offered his arm to Amanda and she smiled as he proudly escorted her into the courthouse behind Sarah and the sheriff.

Miles away, Don Street sped down an empty back road with a dark fury raging in his eyes. "You changed the game," he hissed and struck the dashboard with an iron fist. "You changed the rules, Detective Garland. Now we'll play a different game!"

CHAPTER FIVE

Sarah sat down in a wooden chair by an old wooden desk worn down with time. The desk was tucked into an office that was no bigger than a broom closet, and the papers on the desk were mostly coated with dust, speaking of the boredom and laziness that pervaded the entire courthouse. "Nice office," she said, examining the dark paneled walls. The wood paneling stopped at a green linoleum floor that was cracked and tired.

Paul waved a hand at Sarah and brushed off her comment. "An office is an office," he said and hurried past Amanda and Nate.

Sarah waited until Paul sat down behind his desk before continuing. "I wasn't being insulting," she promised.

"Who cares if you were," Paul replied and yanked out the

top right-hand drawer of the desk and pulled out a blank business card. "Here," he said and slid the card across his desk. "Take it and...do whatever you see fit."

Sarah reached forward, took the card into her hands and examined it. A cell phone number was scribbled on the front of the card. "Can I use your phone?" she asked.

Paul pointed at the brown phone on his desk. "Don't involve me," he said and stood up. "Detective, I became Sheriff of Prate not because I cared about any high-minded ideals about the law," he said in a tired voice. "I became Sheriff because everyone in my family always thought of me as a coward. I wanted to prove them wrong...guess I didn't. My point is, I don't have the training you do...and the murder of your friend scared me to the bone. You're a well-known name in Los Angeles. You tracked down and caught the Back Alley Killer for crying out loud. I've never caught a real criminal in my life." Paul shook his head as if shame soaked his heart. "You have to catch this killer...please," he begged. "But...don't ask for my help. Because I'm going home right now and taking my wife away from Prate until you solve this case."

"Oh, Paul," Nate said in a disappointed voice. "You can't run."

"Your wife wasn't threatened, Nate," Paul retorted in a tortured voice. "My wife...she's all I got. Now..." Paul looked at Sarah. "My office is your office...just...get to work," he finished and ran out of the office and vanished down the hall.

"He's scared," Sarah told Nate, whose face had hardened in the wake of the sheriff's abrupt exit.

"Scared or not, man should never run from a fight," Nate replied and pushed the door shut. "You gonna call the killer?"

"Not yet," Sarah told Nate and picked up the phone. She dialed Pete's cell phone number. Pete picked up on the fourth ring. "Hey partner."

"Don't talk to me," Pete barked.

"Pete, I know you're mad but—"

"Yeah, I'm mad," Pete retorted and stood up behind his desk, grabbed a cigar, shoved it into his mouth, and began walking around his crowded office. "I thought we were going to be partners again."

"We are, Pete," Sarah promised. "Pete, you trained me to think smart and I am being smart. I just found out that the killer wants me back in Los Angeles. Rebecca's murder wasn't a warning to stay away after all."

Pete gnawed on his cigar. "That doesn't make any sense. If the killer wants you back here, why didn't he just wait until you arrived?"

"I'm chewing on that question myself, Pete," Sarah

confessed. "I'm not even sure how the killer knew my location. I'm thinking he tracked my cell phone somehow? That's about the only logical explanation I can come up with."

Pete stopped pacing his office and focused his eyes on the worn carpet floor. "I ordered Sheriff Bufford to run you out of town, you know."

"I know."

Pete shook his head. "Bad move on my part. I let my emotions overwhelm my brains. Seems like staying in Prate was the right thing to do after all. Sorry I jumped down your throat, kid."

"No harm done," Sarah smiled, relieved. "Now listen, Pete, you're not the only one who ordered Sheriff Bufford to run me out of Prate. The killer paid Sheriff Bufford a visit at his home last night."

"Oh?" Pete asked. Sarah dashed out Sheriff Bufford's story. "And you have the number this punk gave Sheriff Bufford?"

"Holding the card in my left hand as we speak," Sarah said. "Pete, run the number for me."

Pete ran over to his desk and snatched up a pen. "Okay, kid, give the number to me." Sarah read off the number to Pete. "Yeah, that's a Los Angeles cell phone number," he said. "I'll run the number and get back to you and...oh, before I forget. I ran Mrs. Diane Samton, the woman who was supposed to meet with you from the big studio?"

"Oh good," Sarah said. "What information came back on her?"

"The woman's dead," Pete told Sarah. "She's been dead since 1973."

"Dead?" Sarah asked, stunned.

"Diane Samton was a two-bit actor in a few films," Pete continued. "She died of lung cancer at the age of seventy-four." Pete puffed on his cigar. "She was married five times, never had a kid, owned a little art studio, nothing major."

"No criminal history?"

"Not even a single parking ticket," Pete shrugged. "Woman was clean as a whistle. Lousy at love, but clean as a whistle."

"Pete, can you find out if—"

"If the movies she acted in were funded by J&P Brothers? Already did and the answer is yes. But that's as far as I got."

Sarah felt confusion grip her mind. "Keep digging, Pete. In the meantime, I'm going to go get my jeep and drive around some. I doubt our killer raced back to Los Angeles."

"I'll let you know if I find something," Pete told Sarah. "Right now, I'm running every gray BMW in the state."

"Remind me to give you a big kiss," Sarah smiled. "Pete, you're my hero."

"I just want you home, kid," Pete sighed. "I was kinda excited about the whole idea of getting you reinstated."

"I know," Sarah apologized. "Tell you what, after this case is solved, Amanda and I will still drive down to Los Angeles and stay a full week. By then, you should be sick of us."

"Deal," Pete smiled and then toughened his tone. "Get to work Detective Garland, and watch your backside," he said and ended the call. "That kid weighs heavy on my heart," he whispered and went back to work himself.

Sarah set down the phone and then stood up. "Okay, Pete is running the number. In the meantime, I want to go and get my jeep and drive around and search for the BMW. The killer has to be staying somewhere."

Nate rubbed his chin. "So what makes you think that boy's still in town?" he asked Sarah.

"It's the nature of a killer," Sarah said in a serious voice. "Nate, whoever he is, he's already killed once and he's bound to keep killing until he's either caught or killed himself."

"But why the games?" Amanda asked and cuddled

Mittens to her chest. "Los Angeles, love, I don't understand what's really happening, even though this is all playing out right before my eyes. If this creep wanted you in Los Angeles, why didn't he wait until you arrived?"

Sarah shrugged her shoulders. "I don't really know, June Bug. I wish I did. I wish I knew how Rebecca was involved. I believe Rebecca was killed because she came across something or someone that—" Sarah paused.

"What?" Amanda asked, reading the startled expression on her best friend's face.

"Diane Samton," Sarah whispered. "Rebecca was a very sharp woman. I wonder..."

"Wonder what?" Amanda pressed.

"Give the woman time to get her thoughts straight," Nate told Amanda in a polite tone.

Sarah closed her eyes. "I called Rebecca yesterday morning...she wasn't in her office. Rebecca is always in her office. When I talked to her, she seemed normal...but her voice...there was something in her voice..." Sarah opened her eyes. "The killer went after Sheriff Bufford...is it possible he was holding Rebecca as his prisoner? For leverage against me?" Sarah closed her eyes again. "What if...Rebecca found out who Diane Samton really was?"

"Why? What did Pete find out about this Diane Samton?" Amanda asked.

"A woman who died over forty years ago of lung cancer. She played a few minor roles in some J&P Brothers movies," Sarah explained. She opened her eyes again and looked at Amanda. "Or, could it be...could it be that...Rebecca was involved with the killer somehow?" she dared to ask.

"You tell us," Nate said to Sarah, baffled. "You're the detective."

Sarah drew in a deep breath. "No, absolutely not," she said in a stern voice. "Rebecca would never betray me." Sarah forced her brain to think. "Rebecca acted in a few movies herself in her younger years...small-time films, nothing major. I wonder...if the name Diane Samton surfaced in her mind somehow...and she realized it couldn't be Diane Samton coming to meet with us from the studio...and that's why the killer went after her?"

"Keep talking," Nate told Sarah. "Work it all out in your mind, girl."

Sarah focused on Rebecca in her mind. "What if the killer believed Rebecca sent me a message to stay out of Los Angeles and—" the phone rang on Paul's desk. Sarah bit down on her lower lip and snatched up the phone. "Hello, this is acting homicide Detective Garland," she said.

"Yes, this is Dr. Alda," a cold voice told Sarah. "Let me speak to Paul."

"Paul is not available," Sarah replied. "Dr. Alda, did you perform an autopsy on Rebecca—"

"Yes, yes, the woman found in Prate," Dr. Alda rudely interrupted Sarah. "Did you say you were a homicide detective?"

"Yes."

"It figures," Dr. Alda snorted. "Well, I'll admit Paul could use the help on this one. As long as you big-city detectives don't stick around acting like you know everything when in fact you're a bunch of outsiders wasting time on the taxpayer's dollar—"

"Doctor please, the autopsy," Sarah cut in. "What did it show?"

Dr. Alda snatched up a cup of coffee and drained it. "The woman's cause of death was a lethal dose of a drug used to put animals to sleep...and I don't mean to dream, detective."

"What's the name of the drug?"

Dr. Alda gave Sarah the name of the drug used to kill Rebecca and explained he had found the injection mark on her skin. "I also found signs of a violent struggle. There were bruises and lacerations on the torso, face, arms and legs. I found skin under the fingernails, which shows how violent the struggle was. But the struggle probably ended when her killer sedated her with chloroform. I found heavy traces of chloroform in the woman's lungs and bloodstream, along with the drug that ended her life."

Sarah felt tears begin falling from her eyes. "Thank you, Dr. Alda."

"Don't thank me for nothing," Dr. Alda objected. "You just find the man who killed this poor woman," he said and hung up without ceremony.

Sarah set down Paul's phone and wiped at her tears. "Autopsy report shows that Rebecca was attacked, probably kidnapped, and drugged to death," she explained.

"Oh dear," Amanda gasped.

Nate shook his head. "Shameful," he grunted.

Sarah wiped at her tears again and called Pete. "Pete, Rebecca's autopsy report just came through," Sarah said, struggling for a moment to control her voice. Then she told Pete every word Dr. Alda had said.

"Okay, kid, I'm going to give the doc a call myself and get a hard copy of the report faxed over. I'll also run a check on the drug used to kill Rebecca and see what I come up with."

"Have her body returned back to Los Angeles, Pete, and contact her nearest family member," Sarah said.

Pete heard tears in Sarah's voice. "You always did take this job hard, kid. I know you were close to her, too. I'll make the necessary calls. Watch your backside, as always."

Sarah promised Pete that she would stay safe and hung up. She walked back outside into the fresh morning air of Prate with Amanda by her side, the puppy in her arms, and Nate trailing them protectively. "Nate, drive us down to the garage, please. I want to get my jeep and look around."

Nate folded his arms together. "Sarah," he said in a clear and urgent voice, "we got a killer to catch. Now, you better clear your brain, girl."

"My brain is clear," Sarah promised. She took a deep breath and willed her emotions about Rebecca's death to wait until later.

"Good," Nate said, seeing her resolve. He watched Amanda climb into the passenger side of his truck with Mittens. "Now, you better start asking yourself what the killer might be thinking right about now."

Sarah looked at the little stores empty and sleeping on Main Street. Prate might feel like an emptying, dying town, but it was also a quiet, small community filled with people who lived simple lives and raised good families. Now, because of her, a deadly killer was loose and casting a dark shadow over the town. "Well, a few of my questions are answered," she said. "I think the killer kidnapped Rebecca because he believed she had warned me to stay out of Los Angeles. Rebecca was probably in the killer's car when I called her."

"That's awful," Amanda said, horrorstruck. But she knew her best friend needed to keep working out the details. "Keep talking," she urged.

"I'm still not sure how the killer knew my location," Sarah confessed.

"Cell phone?" Nate asked.

"That's what I'm thinking," Sarah replied. "The killer had to have tracked my cell phone."

"Is that possible?" Nate asked.

"Anything is possible," Sarah said in a miserable voice. "Sheriff Bufford said the killer is practically a kid. Kids are smart today, Nate. It's not like when you were growing up. Today, kids are raised with every kind of technology you can imagine. I've seen four-year-old babies who can text people."

Nate listened to Sarah with careful patience. "So this kid is talented with those little machines people keep in their pockets all the time."

"It's very possible he's not only talented, but extremely

skilled," Sarah pointed out.

"So all the better to stay where the noise of the world can't touch you," Nate said and motioned around with his arms. "Prate may be small, girl, but she ain't noisy. You tossed your cell phone and you drive a jeep that ain't new or nothing fancy. So you just keep staying in the dark and make this dangerous kid seek you out, because right now, he don't have a clue as to where you're gonna be."

Sarah stared at Nate. The old man's logic was amazing in her eyes. "Nate, you're a brilliant, brilliant, man."

"Nah, just used to letting common sense do my thinking for me. You shot out the windshield to that fancy car and scared off that boy for a bit. Sheriff Bufford is running out of town like a scared cat. You've got a few hours to think and make a plan just as long as you stay in the shadows instead of stepping back into the spotlight."

Sarah bit down on her lower lip and looked at Nate's truck. "Amanda, we're going to walk down to the garage and leave Nate's truck here."

Amanda made an exasperated face—she had expected this—and jumped out of the truck with Mittens. "Let me guess, we're not going to be driving around in your jeep either, right, love?"

"Nope," Sarah said and patted Mittens on her head.

Nate smiled. "That's my girl."

Sarah decided to rent a rundown truck from a man improbably named Furrow Brown. Furrow Brown owned the local garage in Prate, and he was a nice enough fella who thought Sarah was mighty pretty. Of course, Furrow was sixty-nine years old and allowed himself to flirt with young women who in return smiled a pretty smile at him. Sarah was no exception. "Now, the fourth gear sticks some," Furrow told Sarah in a warm voice.

Nate rolled his eyes. "Furrow Brown, you ain't never gonna change," he chuckled.

"Who says I want to," Furrow winked at Nate and smiled over his shoulder at Amanda. "Being a little old man can be fun sometimes."

Amanda grinned. She liked Furrow. "I bet."

"You're just a baby," Nate told Furrow.

"Maybe in your eyes, but my body sure tells me different," Furrow corrected Nate and focused back on Sarah. His face grew serious. "Word around town is there's been a killing. Is that so?"

Sarah kept her eyes on the run-down truck and then stuck her head into the driver's seat and studied the tricky gear shift. The inside of the truck smelled like oil and gas. "Mr. Brown, who told you that?" she asked.

Furrow shrugged his shoulders. "Word gets around," he said and glanced up at the morning sun. The parking lot in front of his garage was deserted. Only oil stains and a few loose tools greeted them when they had walked up. Most folks were staying home because of the murder and those who were brave enough to venture out didn't need their cars fixed. "Word gets around," he said again and let his eyes fall on a vacant lot across the street. He spotted a few stray cats playing around a used tire.

"I see," Sarah said and stood back up. "I'll take this truck, Mr. Brown. I don't know how long I'll need it, though. But in the meantime," Sarah said in a careful voice, "I need you to drive my jeep to a discreet location and park it."

"Sure enough?" Furrow asked and hitched up his gray work slacks.

"Please," Sarah urged Furrow, "be careful. After you hide my jeep, drop off my keys at the courthouse with a note detailing the location of my jeep."

"Sure enough?" Furrow asked again. "Real spy stuff, right here in Prate."

"I'll get the luggage out of your jeep," Nate told Sarah and rolled his eyes at Furrow. "Spy stuff...good grief."

Amanda giggled and handed the puppy to Sarah. "I'll help Nate with our luggage," she said and gave Sarah a desperate look. "Please, love, I want a shower and a fresh dress."

"Me too," Sarah assured Amanda. Amanda sighed a breath of relief and hurried over to the jeep and began helping Nate. "Mr. Brown, there has been a murder," Sarah told Furrow, "but the woman who was killed was from Los Angeles. The killing is not connected to Prate in any way. Unfortunately, Prate was caught in the middle."

"Sure enough?" Furrow repeated and rubbed the scraggly whiskers on his chin. "Well, a little excitement sure ain't gonna hurt this sleepy old town none," he told Sarah. "Folks need to be shook up every now and then."

Sarah looked past Furrow toward his greasy garage. The poor man sure needed some business, but wasn't bound to fix a single car anytime soon. "Please be careful hiding my jeep," she told Furrow.

"Old Furrow Brown is a clever man," Furrow tipped a wink at Sarah. "And Old Furrow Brown has seen that gray BMW driving around this morning, too. I ain't stupid, Detective. I know what to keep my eyes peeled out for, you don't have to worry your pretty little face one little bit."

"Thank you, Mr. Brown," Sarah said in a relieved voice. She hated to ask the man to place his life in danger, but she needed a distraction.

Furrow winked at Sarah again. "Call me Furrow," he smiled.

"Furrow it is," Sarah smiled back and jumped into the truck with Mittens and slid into the middle of the seat. Five minutes later, Nate had the truck moving back toward his house. "Air feels nice," Sarah said, adoring how the gentle spring wind came in through the rolled-down windows and played in her hair.

"Yep," Nate said with his elbow hanging out of the window.

"Sure does," Amanda agreed.

Sarah settled Mittens in her lap. "The killer fired blanks at us yesterday not because he was trying to scare me out of Prate," she explained. "I can see that now. He could have fired live bullets, though."

"Why does this guy want you back in Los Angeles so bad?" Amanda asked.

"Good question, bug. I think we're going to find some of our answers hidden under the doormat at J&P Brothers," Sarah replied. She scratched Mittens' ears. Mittens dropped her head down onto Sarah's lap and drifted off to sleep.

"But...we're in Prate," Amanda said, confused.

"Yes, we are," Sarah said in a grateful voice and smiled at Nate. "When we drive back into town later today, I'm going to call J&P Brothers and ask a few questions. My gut is telling me this mess is somehow related to the dead stuntman."

"What stuntman?" Nate asked.

Sarah slowly explained about the case from her past involving the J&P Brothers. "I never did solve that case, Nate, and had to toss it into the cold files." Sarah looked out of the passenger's window at an open farm field rolling by. She spotted a man on a tractor working the field. The sight of the farmer was soothing to her eyes. "Rebecca told me J&P Brothers were interested in turning my books into movies. We now know that the killer was just setting a trap to lure me to Los Angeles. However, I don't think the killer expected Rebecca to be so sharp-minded. It caused him problems."

"I hate to say this, love," Amanda said in a regretful tone, "but Rebecca might have saved our lives by dying."

"She was a martyr. Like Jesus," Nate nodded. "He who died so we could live."

"Amen to that," Sarah agreed. She looked at Amanda and considered her words. "Maybe?"

Amanda continued. "I was thinking about why the killer didn't just kill Rebecca in Los Angeles. He could have, you know. But instead, he seemed very determined to use her death as some kind of a sick statement. It's like...well, in my mind, he was flexing his muscles at you...his intellectual prowess."

"Makes sense to me," Nate agreed. "Kid likes to show off and make a point."

"And the killer wanted to prove to me that he was in charge," Sarah said. "Maybe he never planned to kill Rebecca, but used her death to his advantage—at least, that's what he might have thought. It's hard to tell what a killer is really thinking, guys. But it does seem Rebecca threw a kink into the killer's plan and forced him to improvise."

"Whatever trap this jerk had laid out," Amanda said, "it's all wrapped up in a nice, tidy little box in Los Angeles."

Sarah agreed. "That's why the killer is trying to force me back there," she replied. "It's starting to make sense in my mind now, more so than last night."

"Only natural for the mind to work out the rough spots over time and clear up the fog," Nate explained. "You ladies had a poison pie thrown in your face all at once and now you're wiping the filling out of your eyes and seeing a little more clearly."

"Speaking of seeing more clearly," Sarah told Nate and pointed to an approaching speed limit sign, "that's about where I threw my cell phone out. Pull over, okay?"

Nate eased the truck off the road and studied the wooded

area. "Okay," he said and opened the driver's side door, "everyone out and look for one of them small phones."

Sarah set Mittens down on the seat and climbed out of the truck with Amanda. Together they followed Nate over to the wood line and began searching through the tall, lush green grass there. Sarah walked over to a thick pine tree, squatted down, and ran her hand through the grass. In larger cities, the grass would have been littered with cans, trash, and cigarette butts. But out in the country, the land was clean, untouched by urban indifference. "I'm sure I threw my phone in this area," she said.

Nate bent down and examined the grass and then began searching behind trees. Amanda began hopping around in a squatted down position, looking for all the world like a grasshopper as she jumped from one location to the next, keeping her eyes peeled on the ground. "Nothing yet, love."

Sarah narrowed her eyes and began crawling around, feeling through the grass, looking behind trees, and then backtracked her movements. Nate eventually walked over to Sarah and shook his head. Amanda joined him. "If only I hadn't walked out of my cabin and forgot my cell phone," Amanda told Sarah, "I could call your phone so we could follow the sound."

Sarah stood up and brushed grass off her knees. "June Bug, my phone isn't here," she said in a confident voice.

"I'm grateful you forgot your phone. If the killer has my phone, and I'm sure he does, I sure don't want him to find out your number."

"Good point," Amanda said in a quick voice.

Nate brushed dirt off his pants. "You sure that dangerous kid has your cell phone?"

"Pretty sure," Sarah replied. "Come on, let's go."

Sarah walked back to the truck and jumped in. An hour later, after taking a long shower and changing into a fresh dress in a shade of pale green, she walked into Nate's kitchen, made herself a cup of coffee, and sat down at the kitchen table. "Amanda is changing...for the hundredth time," she told Nate with a grin.

Nate sipped his coffee. "She's a faithful friend," he said in a pleased tone. "Friends like her become like a sister to you real quick."

"I know," Sarah smiled and thought of Amanda's silly and beautiful face. "She's a very special treasure. I've...placed her life in danger quite a few times...and she still stands by my side."

"That's because she loves you," Nate smiled. "And you love her. You two are sisters at heart, Sarah. And that is a gift from the Lord."

"I know," Sarah agreed. She looked down at her coffee

and then back up at Nate. "Amanda was worried I might move back to Los Angeles."

"Yep."

"I could never leave her," Sarah confessed without realizing that Amanda had walked into the dining room and stopped to listen. "When my husband divorced me, I felt...well, I felt it was time to make a change in my life. So," Sarah took a sip of her coffee, "I relocated to Alaska. Why? Maybe I was searching for a place to hide and lick my wounds."

"Most likely," Nate agreed.

"I met Amanda in the little town I relocated to and we've been close ever since. She's been amazing, Nate. I can't tell you how many tears that woman has wiped out of my eyes," Sarah explained in a loving voice. "If it hadn't been for Amanda...I call her June Bug...I don't think I would have made it through my divorce."

"Amanda is a special lady."

Sarah thought back to the menacing snowman she found standing in her front yard one day, the case that had started it all and brought her and Amanda together. She told Nate about the case and working with Conrad. "That crazy model was going to kill both me and Conrad. Just when I thought we were going to die, Amanda appeared and slugged the model in her face and saved our lives. She's been a real hero, all the way. I owe her so much, Nate. I wish I...I wish I could tell Amanda how much I love her."

"You don't have to," Amanda said and stepped into the kitchen with tears in her eyes. "I already know," she said and held out her arms.

Sarah felt tears slip from her eyes, stood up, and hugged Amanda as tight as she could. "I'm so grateful for you, June Bug."

"As I am for you," Amanda whispered and hugged Sarah back. "When we get home, we'll work on your coffee shop and make it real spiffy and then we'll go shopping at O'Mally's and eat at the diner and watch romantic comedies and paint each other's nails and...oh, all kinds of girly stuff."

"Sounds wonderful," Sarah said, laughing and wiping at her tears. But first, we're going to have our all-girls road trip, June Bug. I'm taking you to Los Angeles and we're going to shop until we drop."

Nate smiled. It sure was great to see the two women bond within their hearts. "I got us cabbage and cornbread cooking. We'll eat before we drive back into town. Old Nate needs his nourishment."

Amanda straightened out the dark blue dress she had finally chosen and sat down. Her hair was still wet from the hot shower but that was just fine with her. "I'm hungry," she admitted and rubbed her tummy. "My, that cabbage smells good."

"Salt, cayenne pepper and ground hamburger meat," Nate said in a proud voice. "Old Nate knows how to make his cabbage stew just right."

"Cayenne pepper?" Amanda asked and looked at Sarah with worried eyes.

Sarah winced. An old-timer like Nate was likely to add more than just a dash of cayenne pepper to his cooking. "Uh...sounds good. By the way, you do have some more of that delicious tea, right?"

Nate read Sarah's and Amanda's worried faces. He let out a loud chuckle. "Old Nate isn't going to set you ladies on fire. I went easy on the cayenne pepper, don't worry."

Sarah and Amanda breathed a sigh of relief. But when Nate served them lunch, their faces turned hot as the red pepper seasoning and their mouths spit out fire. "Hot...hot," Sarah shrieked on the first bite and grabbed her cold glass of tea.

"On fire," Amanda cried and went for her glass of tea, too.

Nate sampled the cabbage stew. "Why, I can barely taste any cayenne at all," he said and shook his head. "Folks just don't know how to eat," he said and took a big bite of cabbage and chased it down with a bite of cornbread. He grinned at them. "Chase it with cornbread, ladies, it helps to tame the fire better than tea."

Sarah wiped tears from her eyes and drained her glass of tea anyway. "Whew," she breathed, "if my mind wasn't clear before, it is now."

"On fire," Amanda continued to cry and finished off her tea, ignoring Nate in her panic. "More tea...more tea." Sarah quickly refilled Amanda's glass as Nate mumbled to himself.

———

Don Street jumped up onto the hood of the gray BMW he had pulled under a thick strand of trees and examined Sarah's cell phone. "Okay, Detective Garland, let's see who is going to be my next victim," he hissed and began searching through the phone's contact list. Conrad's name appeared.

CHAPTER SIX

Sarah walked into the courthouse with Amanda and Nate feeling as if her mouth was going to turn into ashes. But concern over her scorched mouth quickly fled when a fat, uniformed man with a rude expression on his face marched out of Sheriff Bufford's office and slammed the door. The man eyed Sarah and slowly rested his hand on a gun sitting on his hip. "You the woman detective?" he asked in a gruff voice.

"I'm Detective Sarah Garland, yes," Sarah said and examined the man's name tag which was hanging crooked on his brown uniform. "Deputy Jones?"

"That's my name," Heath Jones said and checked Amanda and Nate out. "Nate, why are you dealing with the likes of them?"

Nate pointed at Heath's baggy, unshaven jowls and the

telling bloom of busted capillaries on his nose. "You've been drinking again, Heath. Shame on you. Your daddy was a fine preacher, son, and you ain't doing nothing to honor his name."

Heath raised his right hand and felt his face. Shame entered his eyes. "Yeah, well, life's tough sometimes," he said and tossed a stiff thumb at Sheriff Bufford's office. "You have a...visitor...waiting for you...Detective," Heath said in an acid voice and walked off down the long hallway.

Sarah looked at the closed office door with apprehension. "You two," she whispered, "get down the hallway and stay out of sight."

"No way," Amanda whispered back. "We're a team."

"That's why I want you out of sight," Sarah whispered in a quick voice. "Now go."

Nate took Amanda's arm. "Move," he ordered her and ran Amanda down the hallway and ducked behind a soda machine.

Sarah took out her gun, bravely drew in a breath, and then walked into the office. She saw a young man and her heart nearly stopped.

Don Street was sitting behind Paul's desk with his feet propped up. He looked just like Paul had described, minus the baseball cap. "I thought it was time for us to finally meet," he said in a voice that made Sarah's skin turn cold.

"Maybe," Sarah replied, keeping her gun at her right side. "Who are you?"

"Close the door," he ordered Sarah and threw a pencil lazily at the door so that it stuck, point-first, into the wall.

Sarah kicked the door shut with her right foot. "Who are you?" she demanded.

"You're not a bad shot with that gun," the kid told Sarah, ignoring her question as he grabbed a paperclip and began fiddling with it. "You nearly took my head off."

"That's what I was aiming for."

Don made a sour face at Sarah. "You think you're real smart, don't you," he hissed.

"I figured out a few things," Sarah said, examining the young man's face. He was so young, but his face was tough, soulless and covered with acne scars wherever there wasn't an angry-looking pustule. His eyes were vicious and evil—Sarah could barely stand to look him in the eye. She was afraid to see what was behind those eyes.

"Yeah, I kinda made a mess of things, didn't I?" Don asked and threw the paperclip in his hand down onto the desk and snatched up a pen. "Your friend Rebecca...man, she caused me some real problems. I thought I played her real cool, too...guess I messed up."

"Guess you did," Sarah agreed. Being face to face with the killer, it finally dawned on her that she was dealing with an insane death-hungry killer trapped in the mind of a nineteen-year-old kid who still couldn't get a date. No wonder the case threw piles of confusion into her lap. She wasn't dealing with a seasoned killer who controlled every little detail down to the last drop of blood. No, she was dealing with an amateur who assumed he had complete power but was dripping mistakes all over the trail. Sarah noticed the easy, faint ego of assumed brilliance glowing in Don's eyes—the kind of cheap brilliance bought with technology instead of nurtured over years of life experience. The dim gleam she saw in Don's eyes was a brilliance that was arrogant, overconfident and uncontrolled. It was clear Don Street assumed he was above everyone, was smarter than everyone, and controlled everyone. His dangerous delusions were matched with a quick, ill temper fomenting in a homicidal mind. A kid controlled by deadly madness, anger, and a deranged sense of revenge was a dangerous mixture.

She absorbed all this, and let the silence linger for a second more. "Who are you?" she asked him again.

"Let's find out who you know first," Don told Sarah as he threw the pen down, reached into the right pocket of his leather jacket, and yanked out Sarah's cell phone. "Thanks for the gift," he grinned. "Lot of nice people you have on your contact list, too."

"You've been tracking my cell phone," Sarah said, keeping her voice calm.

"People are so stupid," Don hissed at Sarah. "Every cell phone can be tracked by the FBI, CIA, and NSA. They have access through a secret backdoor in the operating system, and through the hardware, and so do I. Your cell phone is nothing but a stupid tracking device. What, did Little Miss Detective think that when she turned off her phone, no one was listening?"

"I assumed you tracked my cell phone." Her mind was racing but she kept a poker face.

"You assumed right," Don said and tossed Sarah's phone down onto the desk. "You can have it back. I have the information I want."

Sarah resisted the urge to shoot Don. Even though he was a killer, he was still a kid in her eyes. "You were trying to find me?"

"Almost caught up to you, too," Don said in an angry voice. "Found your jeep empty with a flat on the side of the road...that's when your friend tried to make a run for it...I had to kill her...I wasn't planning to, not then, anyway. Stupid thing to do. Really messed my plan up."

Sarah had activated her training in interrogation techniques without Don knowing. She understood how to make a person talk and get vital information without triggering their paranoia. She also knew how to roll the dice and take different gambits with each question and then return to a vital detail when they were least expecting it. "Why were you trying to find me? Why not just wait until I arrived in Los Angeles?"

"Because of your stupid friend!" Don growled. "She messed everything up, cop!" Don stared into Sarah's eyes with fury roiling through him. "I know she tipped you off."

"Maybe she did," Sarah said in a calm attempt to manipulate Don.

"Don't play stupid with me, cop. Your friend Rebecca tipped you off after she discovered who Diane Samton was. Man, was it stupid for me to use that name. I didn't think some dumb lady who worked with lame writers would ever kick such a random name back into the light," Don told Sarah. "Guess you live and learn."

"Rebecca was a smart—no, a brilliant woman." She let her expression turn passionate, knowing he was hungry for these petty moments of triumph.

"She's a dead woman now," Don grinned at Sarah. His voice got more intense as he tried to pinpoint her with his stare. "She tried to run...bad mistake. I ran her down..."

he paused, savoring the anguish he thought he read on Sarah's face. He wanted to make it hurt. "But she couldn't escape. And I taught her just who Don Smart really is."

"Don Street?" Sarah asked.

Don stared at Sarah and realized the fatal mistake he had just made. "Listen, cop, I'm not here to make nice with you. Yeah, I messed up pretty bad."

"You had me thinking I was dealing with a pro," Sarah said, her voice heating. She let him hear a small tremor in her voice, though she kept a steel core of control behind the facade. "You killed my friend. You fired blanks at me—"

"I didn't fire blanks at you, stupid," Don said and shook his head at Sarah. "Are you for real? I tried to shoot the truck you were riding in off the road. I was aiming for the driver."

"I didn't find any bullet holes in the truck."

"I never said I was a great shot, cop," Don said and rolled his eyes. "I'm dealing with a real Einstein here."

Could it be that Don was speaking the truth and every single shot he fired at Nate's truck missed? Surely, Sarah thought, at least one bullet would have struck the truck. Don's face was speaking the truth to her, though. The boy fired real bullets at Nate's truck, but happened to be a lousy shot. Sarah shook her head at this fact. Dealing with a nineteen-year-old killer wasn't going to be simple. Her mind was trained to deal with adult killers, but now she was dealing with a messy kid who had her thoughts running a confusing maze filled with one dead end after another. "Okay, so you're not a pro," Sarah told Don, deliberately trying to insult his ego.

"Oh, I'm a pro, cop," Don snapped. "I'm way smarter than you'll ever be. So what if you caught the Back Alley Killer. That guy was a real loser." Don stared at Sarah with lifeless eyes. "You think you're so clever, don't you? Oh, everybody drooled all over you when you caught the Back Alley Killer, didn't they? Detective Sarah Garland was a big hero and everybody wanted to meet the famous woman detective from Los Angeles."

"I was just doing my job."

"Don't feed me that garbage," Don hissed. "I watched a bunch of old news footage, cop. I saw how you were soaking up the attention, standing so pretty, smiling for the camera, answering this question or that question in your fake cop voice."

"Don—"

"Don't call me by my name, cop. You're not worthy," Don warned Sarah.

Sarah knew that Don had some dangerous plan formed in his sick mind, otherwise the kid wouldn't have allowed himself to be cornered in Paul's office. "What do you want from me?"

"Why don't you ask my dad what he wants? We can just dig up his grave and ask his body! After all, his murder was the one single murder you didn't solve, right?" Don snatched his feet off the desk and stomped the floor. "That's right, Ms. Famous, you let one case slip through your hands, didn't you? But nobody knows that now, do they? Nah, no way, Detective Garland's record is spotless!"

"I never claimed my record was spotless. I tried everything within my power to find out who killed—"

"Don't you ever speak his name!" Don yelled and cast his eyes at the office door. "I guess I better keep my voice down, huh? You're the only cop I want in this office. That dumb deputy actually believed I was your son. He might not like finding out the truth."

Sarah glanced over her shoulder and then looked back at Don. "When I worked on that case, no one at J&P Brothers would speak to me. I chased down every lead I could and ended up with zero. I was finally ordered to place the case in the cold files and move on."

"Sure you were," Don said with cold eyes, "because you failed. You failed a good man."

Sarah quickly began putting a few facts together in her

mind. "You would have been around ten years old if I remember correctly."

"Good memory," Don replied and threw his hands together in sarcastic, brief applause. Sarah glanced down at Don's hands and saw that his fingernails were badly chewed.

"I didn't know your dad," she said in a careful voice. "I'm sorry he was killed."

"Take your apologies and shove it, cop."

"What do you want me to do?" Sarah asked and allowed her voice to show fake irritation. "I was assigned to a case, I did everything in my power to find the killer, I failed, and was forced to move on. It happens."

"Not to my dad it doesn't," Don fired at Sarah. "Nobody moves on. That's a lie. Nobody moved nowhere." He shook his head. "You're going back to that rat-infested studio to solve my father's murder, is that clear? If you don't," Don's eyes turned darker than ever, "I'll make you suffer real bad, cop. Don't think I can't, either. I tracked you down, didn't I? I found you in Alaska. I found out that you've been writing a bunch of lies under a fake name, too. I found out that you were connected to that annoying woman who messed up my plan." Don glared at Sarah. "That's when a plan started to form in my mind, you see...a brilliant plan. I needed you to return to Los

Angeles real bad, cop, and I created a way to make it happen. Didn't I."

Sarah shook her head. "Do you really believe that after all these years the person who killed your dad is still at J&P Brothers?"

"Yes," Don told Sarah and nodded with dark fervor. "I know who killed him, too. That person is dead now, unfortunately. Your job is to go back, prove it, and wrap up the case...give my dad peace...the peace he deserves...the peace my mom deserves. I made it real easy for you. All you have to do is find the body and wrap up the case."

"I'm afraid I don't understand," Sarah said and pretended to sound dumb.

"Oh, you're a real Einstein," Don complained.

"I'm just confused, that's all," Sarah replied.

"And you call yourself a cop," Don griped. "Do I have to spell everything out for you?"

"I guess you do, genius," Sarah replied, deliberately pushing Don.

Don's face knotted up. "Don't push it, cop," he warned Sarah. "I hacked your records without breaking a sweat. I hacked your cell phone, your bank records, your business records, the works, cop. It's not even hard. The computer world is jammed full of nerds that I can't stand. That's why I'm studying to be a veterinarian instead...you can trust an animal, but you can't trust people," he snarled.

Sarah made a few mental notes and focused Don back on her original question. "How were you planning to get me to reopen the case? I would have found out that J&P Brothers weren't interested in my books and Rebecca would—"

"Exactly," Don grinned. "You would have found out that you were lured back to your old stomping grounds under false pretenses and demanded an answer. Which means you would have stuck your nose into J&P Brothers' business again and those two bruised fruits would have figured you were attempting to reopen my dad's case."

"Only an amateur bases his plan on so many assumptions. J&P Brothers pressured a lot of powerful people to have your dad's case closed and forgotten. I'm banned from their studio. If I dared come within ten feet of the main gate I would be arrested."

"Not if you received a phone call about a dead body," Don smirked. "What would J&P Brothers do then, huh?"

Sarah could see Don felt proud of himself. She almost felt sorry for the kid. "Don, your plan is full of too many holes," she said in a steady voice. "How do you know I would have even wasted my time with J&P Brothers after I found the truth? I might have turned around and gone home. And even if you called me and tipped me off about where to find a dead body, so what?"

Don stared at Sarah. "Listen—"

"No, you listen," Sarah snapped. "I'm not a homicide detective anymore. I can't just walk into a major studio and reopen a closed murder investigation. Even if you tipped me off I would have called a detective who was on the force."

Don listened as Sarah slashed his plan to shreds. "You—"

"You shut up and listen," Sarah snapped again. "Maybe in your sick, twisted mind your plan was brilliant. And maybe your nerdy computer hacking skills made you feel overconfident. But the truth is, your plan was weak, stupid and pointless. And because of that, an innocent woman had to die because she managed to connect a few dots."

"Your friend called J&P Studios and started asking too many questions. My mom didn't like that—" Don stopped speaking.

"So your mother works at J&P Brothers?" Sarah asked.

Don balled his hands into two tight fists and struck Paul's desk. "Enough," he hissed and stood up. "Here's the deal, cop," he said and reached into the pocket of his leather jacket and pulled out a cell phone.

"I'm not interested in making a call," Sarah said, waiting.

Don held up the cell phone. "I sent every name on the contact list in your phone to a secure email. That email is monitored by my mother." Don lowered the cell phone. "My mother doesn't work at J&P Brothers, cop. My mother, well, let's just say has some dirt on those two old prunes, and they are willing to let my mother have her way."

"Your mother wants revenge for her husband's death?"

"You bet she does," Don said, "and she got it because I killed the man who murdered my dad."

"Are you sure you killed the right person?"

"My mother tracked down the killer," Don assured Sarah. "All I had to do was carry out the dirty work."

"I see," Sarah said and her thoughts raced down a quick, alternate path for a few seconds and then turned back to Don. "Your mother must be a brilliant woman."

"More than you'll ever know," Don told Sarah in a snide, proud voice.

"You said your mother monitors your secure email?"

"Yeah, I did," Don said and fought back a surge of rage, seeming to seethe every time she questioned him. "I sent every name on your contact list to her. And currently," Don grinned, "my mother is gathering information on those people and assigning hired killers to each one."

"I see."

"Do you?" Don's grin widened. "You do as I say or your friends die, cop. If I don't text my mother our code, she'll release the hit men, and your loved ones will be dead within twenty-four hours, tops."

"Did your mother order you to kill Rebecca?" Sarah asked, changing tack.

Don's grin vanished. "Yeah, but I didn't—not immediately..." he faltered.

"Why?"

"Hey, what my mother didn't know wasn't hurting her. I...all she wanted was for my dad's killer to die. I wanted more. I wanted...peace for my dad. I wanted..." Don struggled, the rage crackling under the surface of every word. "I wanted...you to solve his murder because you were part of his death. Can you understand that, cop? Can you? I needed...closure, okay? Get it? I needed closure...my dad needed closure...my mother needed closure...and I didn't want some strange cop jumping into the scene. I wanted...needed...the original actors, get it?"

"Maybe," Sarah replied with the clear understanding that the death of Don's father had driven the kid insane.

"You better, cop, because my mother has enough money to buy California. She knows people who will put a bullet in you for a few measly thousand, too."

"I bet," Sarah said in a sarcastic tone.

"Oh, you think I'm lying?"

"Nope," Sarah told Don. "I'm just wondering what your mother must be thinking about your failed plan right about now."

Don hissed, "She ain't too happy, okay?" Don ran his hands through his black hair. "I messed up, I should have killed that annoying woman when mom first ordered me to...mom told me my plan was stupid, too. I wanted to prove her wrong."

"Guess that didn't go so well," Sarah said and eased back toward the office door. "Or at least, I doubt she'll think so now."

"Hey!" Don snapped, "I'm going to prove to her that my plan was brilliant. But that's not the point. You're going to solve my dad's murder or your friends are going to die, and my mother will come to her senses later! But trust me, she'll dig it, cop, because I'm going to give her one last choice: either she helps me, or I go public with everything I know about her. But don't worry about that...worry about your friends, cop."

Sarah bit down on her lower lip and began wondering if Don was bluffing about his mother hiring hit men. She thought about her contact list, which was practically empty after all; after the divorce she was so alone. At least until Amanda stepped through the door. Of course,

Don couldn't know that seventy percent of the names he emailed his mother were citizens of Snow Falls, Alaska who needed her number for one reason or another—and furthermore, were the kind of Alaskans who would probably give as good as they got from any hired gun who dared show his face. Amanda and Pete were the only contacts she would be truly worried about, not to mention Conrad. If Don was telling the truth, that is. The kid was really mixed up. "Threatening your own mother isn't nice."

"Hey, in this world, a man's gotta do what a man's gotta do. I'm growing tired of my mother insisting my dad's death be kept in the shadows," Don shook his head. "It took years of me nagging her to finally convince her to help me track down dad's killer."

"I see," Sarah said as her mind connected the final dots to her unsolved murder case. "And your mom tracked down the real killer?"

"Yeah, she sure did. Mom took me right to dad's killer, too. The rat was working on a back lot all by himself." Don's eyes turned dark again. "I strangled him real slowly."

Sarah nodded, not betraying her horror at his deeds. Don's mother had most likely been desperately attempting to locate her son and reel in his sick, out-of-control mind so she could control him. But her desperation was not just because of Don's growing thirst for revenge—it was clear to Sarah that Don's mother was somehow involved in the murder of her own husband and didn't want her son to find out the truth. The woman arranged a fake killer to be framed, letting Don carry out a painful revenge on an unsuspecting person, hoping the ringer's death would solve her problems. But unknown to her, Don was making plans of his own—foolish plans he believed were brilliant and foolproof; until Rebecca caused him problems, that was. Now Don and his mother were mired in a tar pit of their own making, each trying to break free but becoming more and more trapped. "I bet you did," Sarah told Don and raised her gun into the air and pointed it at him. "Get your hands into the air."

Don's face went blank. He stared at Sarah with shock. He managed to recover and sputtered, "Do you not understand what's at stake? Put your gun down or your friends die."

"That's a chance I'm willing to take."

Don's face reddened as his rage bubbled to the surface again. "I told you, if I don't text her the code, my mother will—"

"I seriously doubt your mother is assigning a killer to anyone but you, Don," Sarah said flatly. "I don't need your code to confirm that. Put your hands in the air."

Don balled his hands into fists again, impotent with rage.

But his eyes glowed with a furious light born of desperation. "Put your gun down or the old man dies."

Sarah's blood turned cold. "What old man?"

"The old man I found fishing beside the river," Don grinned, his eyes wildly manic. "Real nice guy, too. He was very willing to help me find my way back to my car, seeing that I was lost and all."

Sarah lowered her gun. Don's eyes told her that he was telling her the truth—he meant to kill an innocent person unless she did as she was told. He was a naïve kid, but not naïve enough to go into this without a backup plan, evidently. "Okay, Don, my gun is down."

Don looked up at the window on the wall behind Paul's desk. He grabbed the office chair and slid it roughly up against the back wall, climbed up on the chair, unlocked the window, and looked at Sarah. "Stay in town until I convince my mother to agree to my plan. She will agree. And then you will solve this case and fix what you left broken. If she refuses, well, I'll handle her. But I think she'll come around soon enough. What choice does she have?" Don grinned again. He took her cell phone out of his jacket pocket and slid it across the desk to her. "I'll be in touch, cop. Be prepared to leave, alone. I'll pick you up at a location of my choosing and drive you to Los Angeles. Once we...get home...I'll take you to the dead body and then you'll do your job, got it? You'll pick up where you left off...and this time, do it right or else."

"I'm not authorized—"

"That's your problem, cop. Find a way to get back on the clock again or else," Don warned Sarah. "My dad deserves this...I deserve this. So get your mind right or the old man won't be the only innocent person who's going to die!"

Sarah resisted the urge to shoot Don. There was no telling where Don's victim was hidden. If Sarah shot and killed Don, the victim might never be found. "I'll handle it," she assured Don.

Don reached into his jacket pocket, whipped out a pair of sunglasses, slapped them on, and climbed out of the window. "I'll be in touch," he repeated with a smirk and jumped to the ground below and vanished out of sight.

Sarah kicked Paul's desk in anger. "I bet you will, you little punk," she growled. "But don't worry, I'll be prepared." Sarah hurried out into the hallway and waved at Amanda and Nate.

Amanda ran up to Sarah. "Where is he?" she asked.

"Gone," Sarah said in a frustrated voice. She pointed to Paul's office. "He went out of the window."

"If you didn't stop him, that means something real bad must have gone down," Nate told Sarah and shook his head. "My, my, what a mess this all is."

"I know," Sarah agreed. She put her gun away and

rubbed her eyes. "The name of our killer is Don Street," she said, feeling a headache kick in. "I let him escape because he kidnapped one of the locals," she continued. "An old man he found fishing beside the river in Prate."

"Only man who ever goes to the river with his pole is Mr. Rhodes," Nate pointed out. "Mr. Rhodes goes fishing at the river whether it's raining or snowing, hot or cold, clear or cloudy. Folks around Prate call him The Mailman Fisherman."

"Poor guy," Amanda sighed. "He went fishing and ended up the prisoner of a very sick person."

"Sick is right," Sarah agreed. "We're dealing with a very disturbed and deadly nineteen-year-old kid who thinks he's invincible and brilliant. A kid who crafted a clumsy plan that cost Rebecca her life." Sarah closed her eyes. The image of the deserted cabin in Alaska flashed through her mind once again. She saw the cabin alone, hungry for life and love, calling her name from the deep wilderness of Alaska. "I need to call Pete," she said, shaking her head and trying to focus.

"Wait a minute before you do," Nate replied and gently touched Sarah's arm. "Your friend can wait. Right now, we need to focus on finding Mr. Rhodes, don't we? The man is my age, and despite his fishing, he's known to be a mite fragile. He ain't likely to live through the night, either. Time ain't on our side, girl."

Amanda looked at Sarah with worried eyes and then focused on Nate. "Nate, where would we even look?"

"If that punk found Mr. Rhodes down by the river, that means he has to be hiding someplace near there himself," Nate pointed out. "I ain't about to let some punk kill an old friend."

Sarah saw anger explode in Nate's aged eyes. She began to tell Nate she agreed with him when all of a sudden Nate turned very pale and fainted before their eyes. "Nate!" Sarah cried out and managed to catch his body before he hit the floor.

"No!" Amanda exclaimed and burst into tears as she dropped down onto her knees and pulled Nate's head onto her lap. "Nate...love...speak to me."

Sarah threw her head down on Nate's chest. "He has a heartbeat and...he's breathing," she said in a grateful tone.

"His face is so pale," Amanda cried and gently caressed Nate's face. "Don't die, love...stay with us, please."

Sarah jumped to her feet, ran into Paul's office, and called for an ambulance. Minutes later, everyone working in the courthouse gathered around Nate and waited for the ambulance to arrive. When the ambulance finally did arrive, Sarah was told that only one person could ride to the hospital with Nate. Amanda insisted on being that person. She hugged Sarah, followed the paramedics outside, climbed into the back of the blue and white ambulance, and it sped away, leaving Sarah standing alone. Sarah wiped at her tears and walked back to Paul's office, feeling as if both of her arms had been cut off. When she reached the office, she closed the door and called Pete. "Don Street paid me a visit," she said and wiped at more tears.

Pete heard the tears in Sarah's voice. "What's wrong, kid? Talk to me."

"The kind old man who's been helping me and Amanda just collapsed. He's being rushed to the hospital."

"I'm sorry to hear that," Pete told Sarah and spit out the cigar in his mouth into a metal ashtray on his office desk. "Are you okay?"

"Tired," Sarah confessed. "Pete, we're dealing with a very dangerous, mentally ill kid who is bent out of shape in every direction possible." Pete listened to Sarah explain the encounter she had with Don. "It's clear that Don's mother had him kill an innocent person, Pete. You need to find this woman as quickly as you can."

"I'll look into her," Pete promised, "but if she has the money her son claims she does, slapping handcuffs on her won't be easy and you know that. I need hard evidence, kid. And right now, all I have is a bunch of words."

Sarah rubbed her eyes with her left hand. "I know," she said miserably. "Uh...did the cell phone number show anything?" she asked, trying to remain focused.

"The kid is smart, Sarah...at least with phones. The cell phone he's carrying around is a prepaid phone that was purchased in Mexico."

"I'm not surprised," Sarah replied. "Don Street claims he hacked into my personal records and bank records. I'm sure he has," she told Pete. "He did manage to track me to Alaska and find out I was writing under a penname."

"When our lives are made digital, it's pretty pointless to hope for privacy," Pete groused and snatched up his cigar. "Listen to Pete, kid. You better catch this looney, do you hear me? I'll check on his mother and see what her story is while you're doing your job."

"Pete, I could cause an innocent man to die if I'm not careful," Sarah pointed out. "This town isn't set up to handle a person like Don Street."

"You're a smart kid, too," Pete assured Sarah. "You've handled worse than some lame-brain kid running around with a few screws loose."

"Yeah," Sarah sighed and closed her eyes again. Nate's pale face burst into her mind. "I've handled worse," she agreed, "but I've never dealt with a killer who isn't old enough to buy a bottle of wine, Pete."

Pete chewed on his cigar. The case was a mess and there was no silver lining in sight.

CHAPTER SEVEN

Sarah let her eyes fall down to Nate's pale face. "Now, don't go being sad on account of me," Nate told Sarah in a weak voice. "Old Nate isn't going home to Heaven anytime soon."

Amanda walked around Nate's hospital bed and patted Sarah's hand. "Nate is being flown to Portland in the morning," she explained. "The doctor who came in and spoke with me—some backwoods guy who looked like he was barely out of high school—is sending Nate to a specialist."

"The doctor doesn't know why Nate collapsed?" Sarah asked in a desperate tone. She looked at the IV line in Nate's right arm and the heart monitor attached to his chest. The hospital room Nate was resting in was small and depressing, dominated by dark brown and red colors that mingled with a horrible disinfectant smell.

"Not yet," Amanda replied and rubbed Nate's forehead.

"I've been running myself too hard, that's all," Nate assured Sarah. "I ain't used to running my body so hard. All I need is a little rest and I'll be as good as new, wait and see."

Amanda rubbed Nate's forehead again. "I called Harry. He's on his way."

"Oh, that old fart," Nate complained and then smiled. "I reckon he'll bring his Uno cards."

Sarah studied Nate's face. The old man seemed very weak, yet his eyes were full of life. In her heart, deep down where the truth speaks, she felt that Nate wasn't going to die. This feeling sent relief through her mind. "Nate, I need your help, okay?"

Nate raised his eyes and focused on Sarah. "You want Old Nate to tell you about the river, don't you?" he asked.

"I need to know if there are any caves, abandoned buildings, houses, any place a person could hide that might be near the river," Sarah said, nodding her head. "I'm going to find Mr. Rhodes...alone," Sarah said and looked at Amanda. "June Bug, I want you right here beside Nate. Please."

Amanda began chewing on her lip and then looked down into Nate's eyes. Nate needed her. "Okay, love, I'll stay with Nate," she conceded with a worried voice.

Nate smiled at Amanda and closed his eyes. "Sarah, my girl," he said in a loving voice, "there is an old cave that us kids used to mess around in that's close to the river. The cave isn't that big...more or less a large room."

"Where is this cave?" Sarah asked. Nate kept his eyes closed and slowly began to voice directions to the cave. Sarah whipped out a small notepad from her pocket and wrote down the directions. "What about any abandoned buildings or houses or—"

Nate shook his head. "County went and tore down every deserted place along the river after a hitchhiker fell asleep with a cigarette in his hand and set an old workshop building there on fire back in 1987. Fire nearly made its way all the way into Prate."

Sarah reached down and touched Nate's cheeks. "A girl could truly marry you," she smiled.

"Oh, now," Nate smiled and opened his eyes, "my wife might be a tad jealous."

"Don't worry. I'm jealous of her already," Sarah smiled again. She thought about her plan and looked at Amanda. "June Bug, Don Street is a dangerous killer, I'm not denying that. But he's also a very disturbed kid that's trying desperately to hold a flimsy plan in place."

"No wonder we couldn't make sense of things yesterday," Amanda sighed. "This kid has us grasping at straws looking for logic, but there was no logic in it to begin with."

"Yeah, I know," Sarah agreed. "My main concern is to capture Don Street before he hurts anyone else. Pete is dealing with his mother. We'll have to wait and see what he comes up with. In the meantime, I'm going solo and—" Before Sarah could finish her sentence, a man knocked on the hospital room door. To Sarah's shock, Conrad walked into the room. "Conrad?"

Amanda quickly buried her face in her hands. "I...uh, well, love...at Harry's, when you went to use the bathroom, I...kinda called Conrad and told him what was happening."

Conrad walked up to Sarah and looked into her eyes. "And I took the first flight I could. You should have called me."

Sarah stared into Conrad's eyes and felt relief—if not joy —wash over her. She reached out and hugged Conrad. "Thank you for coming," she whispered.

"Anytime," Conrad whispered and hugged Sarah back warmly. "Amanda told me you were dealing with a serious killer."

Sarah let go of Conrad. "In a way, yes, in a way, no," she said and carefully detailed Don Street's profile for Conrad.

Conrad listened to every single detail and then focused his attention on Nate. "Sir, forgive me, I'm Conrad Spencer."

"Amanda has told me about you," Nate told Conrad and gave him a smile of approval. "Forgive this old man for not shaking your hand. My arms are a bit weak."

Conrad walked over to Nate and took his right hand and shook it. "Always an honor," he told Nate. "When you get back home, you can cook me some of those good beans Amanda bragged to me about."

"That'll be mighty fine," Nate smiled. He saw goodness in Conrad—a goodness that soothed his tired heart. "I'm mighty grateful Sarah won't be going to the river alone, too. I was a whole lot worried about our girl here. Don't matter if this kid is nineteen or a hundred...a snake can strike at any age, and this kid has already struck twice."

"Don Street killed a person he believed had murdered his father and then he killed Rebecca," Sarah explained. "Conrad, his mother set him up to kill his first victim. I believe she did this to appease Don, in the hopes his urge for revenge would settle down afterward. But Don came up with another plan on his own, and it's this plan that's causing all these problems." Sarah ran her hands through her hair with tired hands. "Right about now, I'm positive Don's mother is desperately trying to create another plan that will reel her son in from the dangerous tide he's swimming in. But Don isn't going to fall for false bait. He's determined to carry out his plan, Conrad."

"This kid had our minds all tangled up last night," Amanda admitted.

Sarah laughed wearily to herself. "We thought he fired blanks at Nate's truck...turns out he's just a really bad shot. We thought Rebecca's death was a warning to stay out of Los Angeles. Turns out Don was trying to scare me out of Prate...at least, that's how he saw it in his sick, twisted mind." Sarah looked at Conrad. "We had a hard time figuring out Rebecca's location on the morning I called her, once we figured out she was found dead here the same day...it wasn't until today that we became aware we were slipping and sliding in the mess of a nineteen-year-old kid."

"Sounds fun," Conrad told Sarah.

"Tell that to Sheriff Bufford," Nate piped up. "Poor guy is taking his wife and running as far away from Prate as his legs will carry him."

"Don threatened Sheriff Bufford's wife last night," Sarah explained. "He ordered Sheriff Bufford to chase me out of town, too. But Conrad, this is a small town and the sheriff isn't exactly one of the Hardy Boys. He slipped up this morning when Don sped past the courthouse in his BMW right after we arrived."

"So it was the killer who forced the sheriff to spill the beans on your location, huh?" Conrad asked.

"Yes," Sarah sighed. "Poor man...he was simply scared for his wife. I can't blame him for doing what Don ordered him, Conrad."

"Guess no one can," Conrad agreed and slowly slid his hands into the pockets of his leather jacket. "Well, there's no sense in standing around. We have a killer to catch, Detective Garland."

"I know," Sarah agreed. She looked at Nate. "We'll be back after Don Street is behind bars."

"Or dead," Nate pointed out.

"Or dead," Sarah hugged Amanda. "Stay with him, June Bug."

Amanda hugged Sarah and then hugged Conrad. "Take care of my girl," she whispered.

"You bet," Conrad whispered back and walked out of the room with Sarah. "Are you okay?"

"Just upset," Sarah confessed as they hurried outside into the warm sunlight. "Conrad, Rebecca is dead. I'm still trying to wrap my mind around it. She died...horribly, at the hands of a nutcase. And I haven't yet stopped chasing him long enough to mourn the loss of my friend."

"I'm sure there will be time once this is all over, Sarah,"

Conrad replied and pointed to his black rented SUV, parked in the small parking lot on the west side of the depressingly small one-story hospital. "But for now, focus on this kid. I admit, from what you told me, anticipating this kid's thoughts is like trying to talk to dust bunnies. But that doesn't mean he's not deadly."

Sarah looked around the parking lot. The hospital was surrounded by beautiful trees and lush flower beds—but even nature's beauty couldn't distract her from the horrible events that had led to this day. "Kids today, Conrad...it's not like it was when we were growing up. Don found me because he tracked my cell phone...he's smart in that sense, but then he created a stupid plan that seemed concrete in his young mind. I guess I can deal with that...but I keep thinking...how many future Dons will there be in this world? What is society doing to our children? I managed to track down and capture the Back Alley Killer...an insane but very clever man...but a nineteen-year-old kid had me chasing my tail for the last couple days."

Conrad walked Sarah over to the SUV. "Society is getting worse for our kids, that's for sure. The world is filled with criminals who prey on the innocent...there are social engineering programs disguised as media, movies, music and so on. It's no wonder some parents are starting to object about the injection of poison vaccines into their children. How can you trust figures of authority anymore? There are immoral agendas on all sides that threaten to corrupt the minds of children...it's all out there, Sarah, and it's only getting worse." Conrad shook his head. "While I was driving to this hospital from the airport, I heard some politician on the radio claim she wanted to abolish marriage because it enslaves women. Then I heard another politician state he wanted the government to raise America's children because traditional parental roles were no longer relevant."

Sarah leaned against the back of the SUV and rubbed her eyes. "This world is decaying from the inside out," she said and shook her head. "And all you and I can do right now is chase down a deadly kid who might get a few headlines in some papers before he'll be forgotten."

"That's about it," Conrad agreed. Conrad folded his arms together. "Sarah, from everything you told me, I think this kid went off the rails after his old man was killed. I'm wondering if he saw the murder take place."

"I've thought about that. I've even wondered if...Don killed his own father, somehow."

"How so?" Conrad asked.

"Well," Sarah said, walking her mind back into the darkened set filled with scary houses designed to be used in a horror movie. It was the set where she had been so many years ago for that fateful case. "Don's father was a stuntman, as you know." Conrad nodded. "At the time of his death, he was practicing for a scene in which a man was strangled to death after becoming tangled up in the rope he was going to use to escape his attacker. The scene involved the man running across a roof, tripping over his feet, falling over the roof, and getting strangled to death."

"Nice," Conrad winced.

"That's Tinsel Town for you. The studios create awful violence on the big screen and then cry foul when violence happens in reality," Sarah replied.

Conrad rubbed his chin. "Yeah," he said and looked into Sarah's eyes. "So, are you thinking this kid somehow caused his dad to slip up somehow and kill himself?"

"Maybe," Sarah said. "Conrad, J&P Brothers had every employee at the studio clam up on me. At the time, I was leaning toward placing guilt on their shoulders, that the studio was simply guilty of being negligent and lax about safety precautions, but that never sat well in my gut. I always had the feeling that the real killer...might have gotten away. I couldn't get anywhere with questioning because they had all been ordered to stay quiet, apparently. But when Don told me his mother had some form of power over J&P Brothers, that made me begin to wonder who really ordered everyone to clam up."

"A mother trying to protect her son?"

"Possibly," Sarah explained, and said, "and a mother who knows her son is mentally ill, too."

"I see," Conrad said and went silent for a minute. "And you said the person Don killed recently, the person he believed killed his old man, was nothing more than a fake rat given to a hungry snake?"

"I believe so. I believe Don's mother set up the killing because she was hoping it would settle down Don's agitated mental state. Conrad, I believe Don is wrapped up in guilt and wants to...go back in time, as it were, in order to find peace. He wants the crime scene in its original form. With the original actors, including me."

"The young boy is trapped in his mind and is trying to break free...instead, the killer teenager is caught up in some ropes himself and about to fall off the roof."

"Exactly," Sarah said. "I think it's possible Don caused his father's death and that caused him to go insane. I think his mother found out the truth and protected her son. But through the years, Don's mental state grew worse and worse, finally forcing his mother to create a false killer and hand that person over to her son, hoping to calm him down. What she didn't know was that Don was working on a plan of his own."

"The boy wants to transfer guilt onto another innocent dead man, thinking it will set his mind free."

"Yes," Sarah said. "And in order to do so, he needs everything, the complete scene, to be exactly the way it once was."

Conrad rubbed the back of his neck. "Well," he said and looked up at the sky, "day is getting late. We better start riding and talk on the way."

Sarah pulled out her gun and checked it. "Don killed Rebecca, Conrad. He has to face justice."

Conrad watched Sarah put her gun away. He could see that the case was weighing heavy on Sarah's heart. "Are you okay? Really, are you okay?"

"I just keep thinking...what if I hadn't allowed the murder of Don's father to be tossed into the cold case files? What would have happened if I hadn't just...given up?" Sarah asked in a guilty voice. "Rebecca would still be alive."

Conrad put a gentle hand on Sarah's troubled shoulder. "Sarah, we're only human," he told her. "Back home in Alaska, people are eating at the diner and watching Jeopardy while in New York somebody is probably committing a serious crime as we speak. All we can do is our job."

"If I had done my job in the first place, we wouldn't be in this mess," Sarah replied and walked around the passenger's side door and climbed into the SUV.

***

The river was wide, beautiful and very inviting in the late

spring twilight. The riverbank was lined with healthy, lovely trees, their branches hanging over the river in the lazy dappled light of the sunset. In certain places, the river flowed very deep, while in others you could see a muddy bottom. Some areas of the river had powerful, fast currents while other areas flowed smooth and easy without a care in the world. "I could pitch a tent, start a campfire, roast some hot dogs, and then go fishing all night," Conrad told Sarah, looking at the river as he walked past a tall tree. "This would make a great fishing spot, too."

Sarah paused. Darkness was falling, casting shadows down onto the river. Despite the grave mission that brought them to the river's bank, the shadows weren't ominous. Instead, Sarah felt that the falling shadows were old voices mingling together, talking about the day while they tucked themselves into the waters of the river. "It's very peaceful," she said and looked at Conrad. "Can I confess something to you?"

"Sure."

"I keep thinking about that deserted cabin where we buried Milton's father," Sarah told Conrad. "I don't really understand why. The cabin is really far away from town and very lonely. Yet, I keep feeling drawn to it."

"Really?" Conrad asked in a strange voice. Sarah nodded. Conrad leaned against a tree and looked at the river. "Can I make a confession?"

"Okay."

"I've been thinking about that cabin, too...a lot, as a matter of fact," Conrad confessed. "I actually decided to make a hiking trip back to the cabin next week on my day off."

"Really?" Sarah asked, amazed.

"I'm telling you the truth," Conrad promised. "I have felt...connected to that old cabin for some strange reason. It was like...well, this may sound stupid...but it was like...I belonged with it, somehow."

Sarah stared at Conrad with wide eyes. "Me, too," she said. "I felt like I needed to go back to that cabin for some reason...and bring life back to it. Oh, I'm not saying I want to live there by any means. But, I want to...call it home, too."

Conrad reached down, grabbed a small pebble and tossed it into the river. "I know what you mean," he said. "Maybe when we get home, you and I can take that hike to the cabin together, huh?"

"Sounds good," Sarah agreed, her heart happy at the prospect. She looked around. "According to Nate's directions, we're not too far away from the cave."

Conrad nodded. "About how far?"

"Maybe...half a mile?"

"Okay then," Conrad said, "this is where we split up. I'll follow you and keep out of sight."

Sarah didn't want to leave Conrad, but she knew the time had come to split up. "Okay," she said and pulled her cell phone from the front pocket of her dress. "Don hasn't tried to call me yet. He's most likely waiting until it turns night. We better hurry."

Conrad pulled out his gun. "I'm not going to hesitate to take the shot if the situation calls for it," he informed Sarah. "Your job is to find the hostage."

"Indeed I will," Sarah promised Conrad and pointed down the river and had started walking when her cell phone began to vibrate. She checked the incoming call and felt a flood of relief. "It's Pete. I better take this."

Conrad looked around. "Okay," he agreed.

Sarah answered the call. "Pete?"

"Hey kid," Pete said. "I've been talking with Bonnie Street."

"Don's mother?"

"Yep," Pete said and tossed a half-chewed cigar into the corner of his mouth. "I brought her in for questioning and really placed the iron glove on her."

"What was the outcome?" Sarah asked.

"Woman broke down like a sugar cube in hot water when

I mentioned the death of your friend Rebecca and what the autopsy report revealed. She broke down even more after I told her everything her son had thrown at you...about her finding his old man's real killer...about sending her the names of the people on your contact list...I really laid the guilt on the thick."

"And?" Sarah asked.

"Well," Pete said and chewed on his cigar, "the woman began insisting that she had nothing to do with her son's actions," Pete explained. "Bonnie Street claimed she knew nothing about what her son was doing. She insisted she didn't find her husband's real killer and that Don was lying through his teeth."

"But she's the one lying through her teeth."

"You better bet your lunch on that," Pete grinned. "And speaking of, I'm hungry for some Chinese food."

"Later with the food, Pete," Sarah pleaded.

"Tell that to my stomach," Pete grunted. "Anyway, I'm holding Bonnie Street in custody right now until our guys can go over and check J&P Brothers."

"Expect resistance."

"Not this time," Pete said in an easy voice. "The old J&P Brothers themselves gave me a call and offered their full cooperation. It seems, kid, that this time around they aren't interested in letting a woman who's been rigging their books blackmail them again."

"Oh, so that's what Bonnie Street has over them," Sarah said.

"Her official title is Secretary, but her job was to rig the books," Pete confirmed. "Also, and you're gonna love this, kid, the brothers themselves are willing to testify in court that Bonnie Street has been blackmailing them all these years."

"That will definitely break her," Sarah said, and then an idea came to her mind. "Pete, I just had an idea. I'm close to the cave where we believe Don is holding Mr. Rhodes, the hostage. Conrad is with me."

"That's good," Pete said, relieved that Sarah wasn't alone. It wasn't that he was worried Sarah couldn't handle herself alone, because she was fully capable of tackling a grizzly if the situation called for it—it was just that backup never hurt, and Conrad Spencer had a good reputation as a cop.

"Listen, Pete, have Bonnie Street call her son and inform him that she's been arrested and is confessing to everything, the whole nine yards, the works. That will surely blow Don's plan to pieces and force him to realize that he's failed."

"I'm listening," Pete said.

"Make sure to tell Bonnie Street to mention that the J&P Brothers are going to testify in court against her," Sarah continued.

"Can do, but why do you want to push that punk over the edge when there's a hostage at stake?"

"I want to send him into panic mode," Sarah explained. "Don doesn't know Conrad is lurking out here with me. If I can cause him to panic, maybe, just maybe, he'll run and leave Mr. Rhodes behind and Conrad and I can snatch him outside of the cave instead of having to force our way inside."

Pete considered Sarah's suggestion. "Well, it's worth a shot," he finally said. "I'll go talk with Bonnie Street and get her on the horn to her son."

"Give me a good ten minutes before she makes the call," Sarah said.

"Okay, kid," Pete said. "We're down to the wire on this case. My end is secure, now get your butt in gear and secure your end."

"Will do," Sarah said and ended the call. "Conrad, we have to hurry."

"Looks like we don't need to split up after all," Conrad said and hurried away with Sarah as the last light of day slowly slipped away. "Your plan is risky," he whispered, keeping his feet stealthy and away from branches that might snap and give away their location. "But it's good. I was worried about how you were going to draw Don out of the cave, assuming he's hiding in there."

"Me, too," Sarah confessed. "According to Nate, the cave has only one entrance and that makes it very difficult for us to get in and out unseen and unheard."

"Yep," Conrad said and continued toward the cave with Sarah and came to a stop when he spotted the gray BMW parked under a tree on a narrow dirt lane that looked like it led back to the main road. The BMW was under a tree and well hidden. Conrad bent down behind a tree and studied the area. "There," he said and pointed to a bunch of broken tree limbs covering the mouth of a small cave.

"I see it," Sarah said, squinting through the darkness. Don was nowhere in sight.

"Hang tight," Conrad whispered. Without saying another word, he vanished into the brush, silent as a mouse. He eased over to the BMW, felt the hood, and then made his way back to Sarah. "Hood is cold. Boy hasn't been on the road in the last few hours."

Sarah pulled her gun out. "Pete should be having Bonnie Street make the call any minute now."

"Okay, here's the plan," Conrad whispered, "we're going to situate ourselves behind the cave, okay? When Don comes out of the cave, you'll take him from the right side and I'll take him from the left side. If we hear any screaming from the hostage from within the cave, we charge inside."

"Agreed," Sarah whispered back. She followed Conrad through the brush, positioned her body on the left side of the cave, and waited as silence began to buzz in her ears. A couple of agonizingly slow minutes later, she heard Don's cell phone ring.

Don answered the call. "Yeah, mom, what is it?" he griped. Don's voice echoed up to the entrance of the cave, letting Sarah know that the boy was standing in the back of the cave. Any chance of a surprise attack was minimal.

"Please, let me go," begged a scared, elderly male voice. "I ain't done anything wrong to you, son. Let me go and I won't tell a soul, please."

"Hang on, mom. Shut up, old man," Don hissed. The sound of scuffling reached their ears, as if he had kicked a scree of loose rock towards the old man. "You're going to be dead soon enough, so stop moaning in your drool."

"Please, son," Mr. Rhodes continued to beg, "I ain't never hurt you, have I?"

"Listen, old man," Don hissed again, "I'm going to collect a little package and split town in a couple of hours. When I do, you'll be dead. So stop begging for your miserable life, because it's really starting to annoy me." Don focused back on the phone call. "Look, mom, I don't want to argue with you anymore. Either do what I tell you or I'm going—"

A shaky, female voice interrupted Don. It was loud enough that Sarah and Conrad could plainly hear her words over the cell phone. "I've been arrested, son," Bonnie Street informed Don. "The cops know that you killed Tom and Rebecca."

Don's voice went weak and shaky. "What?" he asked. "No, this can't be...how?" But then he paused. "Detective Garland!" he screamed. "She betrayed me!" Don spun around and they heard the sound of dirt being kicked at Mr. Rhodes again. "I guess your life means nothing to a cop, old man," he roared in a fury.

"Son, please, turn yourself in," Bonnie pleaded with Don, her voice crackling but loud. "The J&P Brothers, Don, they're going to testify against me in court."

"Impossible," Don gritted out in a hoarse growl. "Those two old men wouldn't dare risk their reputation."

"Murder is involved, Don," Bonnie explained in a desperate tone. "It's gone too far. J&P Brothers would rather be fined for rigging their books than have their reputation ruined with murder."

"Impossible!" Don screamed. "I need everything...the scene has to be...everyone has to be in their places!"

"Don, it's over," Bonnie said. "Son, turn yourself in. I've

already told the police everything I know. I told them that you killed Tom and Rebecca. I told them..." Bonnie paused, trying to breathe and steady her shaking voice. "I confessed to setting Tom up to be murdered...oh Don, Tom didn't kill your father. I made you believe he did because you needed to believe that."

"Shut up!" Don yelled at his mother. "Shut your mouth! Shut your lies!"

Sarah listened as Don began to come apart at the seams and cautiously eased her head forward and looked through the broken tree branches covering the cave's entrance. She spotted a small fire burning near the back of the cave. Don was standing near the fire. Unfortunately, the boy was too close to the hostage to get a clean shot. It could very well ricochet and hit Mr. Rhodes, if they weren't careful. "What to do?" Sarah whispered and then had an idea. She leaned back against the left side of the cave and waited.

"Don, we both know it was an accident. Your father was working on the roof of the stage house...all you did was call out his name. It wasn't your fault that he turned around and tripped on the ropes."

"Shut up!" Don hollered. "I didn't kill my dad!"

Bonnie Street sobbed. "I was wrong to cover up his death," she told Don. "I was worried...that the cops might take you away from me."

When Sarah peeked cautiously into the cave again, she saw Don gritting his teeth as he kicked a burning piece of wood out of the fire. The wood flew through the air and struck the left side of the cave wall. "You're lying...this is a trick...the cops don't have you..."

Sarah ducked back behind the branches and then she heard a familiar voice echoing over the cell phone in the cave. "Boy, you're speaking to a Los Angeles Police Department Homicide Detective," Pete said in a stern tone. "I have your mother in cuffs as we speak. Now, you better listen to what your mother is telling you and let us help you before you do anything stupid."

Don hollered at the top of his lungs. "Bring it on, cop!" he threatened Pete and then came the snap of the cell phone as he ended the phone call.

"Now," Sarah said, brought out her cell phone, and called Don.

Don answered almost immediately. "So it's you," he hissed. "You betrayed me, cop, so now the old man dies."

Sarah carefully moved away from the cave in order to hide her voice. "Don, give it up," she said. "We're mobilizing our forces as we speak. Even if you kill the hostage, there's no chance of escape. Don't add a third murder to your record."

Don was silent. Sarah could hear his breath quickening as panic took over his anger. His plan had failed and now he would be forced out of attack mode and into survival mode. "I'm not afraid of you, cop."

"Don, we know you're hiding in a cave and we know the location of the cave. We're going to be at your location in less than ten minutes. The main roads are being blocked off. There's no chance of escape. Please, give yourself up before anyone else gets hurt."

Don swallowed loudly. "I can escape on foot," he yelled at Sarah in desperation. "I'm not going down without a fight!"

"Don, you killed two innocent people. We're not going to let you escape," Sarah promised.

"Come and get me, cop!" Don yelled and she heard a smashing sound that told her he had thrown his cell phone up against the cave wall and smashed it.

Don stood very silently as panic and fear swallowed his mind. "What am I going to do now?" he whispered and looked toward the cave's entrance where hope stood dark and fleeting.

CHAPTER EIGHT

Sarah motioned at Conrad to work his way over to her. Conrad carefully peeked his head around and took a look inside the cave and then moved around to Sarah. "Okay, so you have the boy freaking out. Now what?" he whispered.

"We'll stand out here until he makes a run for it," Sarah whispered back, feeling the chill envelop them as the heavy drape of night fell on her shoulders.

Conrad threw his left thumb at the BMW. "He's most likely still going to make a run for his car," he told Sarah. "I'll go hide behind the hood. You take that tree over there."

"Got it," Sarah agreed. Conrad smiled at her, gently touched her chin, and moved into position. Sarah hurried to a large tree close to the BMW, reluctantly moving out of hearing distance from the cave. She only hoped that he would take the bait and flee, and not take out his anger on the old man.

"Please," Mr. Rhodes begged Don, "let me go, son. I ain't ever done nothing to hurt you."

Don swung around and cast his deadened gaze at the old man he had tied up. Suddenly, the old man seemed like a liability instead of a valuable pawn on the chessboard. His mind warned him that if he killed the old man, the authorities would set every man and woman in the state on a manhunt for him. "I can't take him hostage because he'll slow me down," Don muttered in a jittery voice and began pacing around the cave. "I gotta move. Police are on their way. Gotta think—"

"Please, son," Mr. Rhodes begged. "Let me go."

"Shut up!" Don tried to holler. Only his voice came out in a scared, strangled groan instead of a threatening bellow. "I need to think, so just shut up!"

Mr. Rhodes swallowed. He could clearly see that his captor was panicking, and panicking wasn't a smart road to take. Panic made a man to make stupid and rash decisions. So he decided to be smart and throw one last plea into the air. "I know another way out of this cave, son."

"What?" Don asked. He ran over to Mr. Rhodes, bent down, and grabbed him by his shirt collar. "Where?"

"Over there," Mr. Rhodes nodded towards the far back corner of the cave. "There's a little tunnel under that rock."

Don looked over at a rock about the size of a kitchen table. The rock seemed a normal part of the rock wall in his eyes. He hadn't thought about a second entrance being hidden anywhere inside the cave. As far as he could tell, the cave had one entrance and one exit. "Don't lie to me, old man," he growled in Mr. Rhodes' face.

"Go see for yourself. Us kids used to play in the tunnel before the men in town pushed that rock over it and threatened to tear our backsides off if we ever stepped foot in this cave again." Mr. Rhodes shook a little with Don's livid face threatening him so closely.

Then Don bolted to his feet, ran over to the rock, and shoved the rock forward with all the panic-fueled strength he could muster. A cold draft shot up from a dark hole and struck him square in the face. "Where does this lead to?" he demanded.

"Out to the river," Mr. Rhodes explained. "Tunnel twists and turns some...goes for maybe a quarter of a mile, if I remember right. You'll have to crawl on your belly or walk low on your knees, son."

Don bit down on his lower lip. He felt hope surge back

into his panicked chest. "Old man, you just saved your life," he said and quickly yanked a penlight from his jacket pocket and put his gun at the ready. "Somebody will be along shortly to untie you," he said nonchalantly and without wasting another breath, he slithered into the dark tunnel.

Mr. Rhodes breathed a sigh of relief and began fidgeting with the ropes holding his wrists and ankles together. He was an old man, but he wasn't weak. Besides, the boy who had tied him up wasn't very experienced in knot tying. Mr. Rhodes was. After serving four years in the Navy he had learned to tie a whole bunch of different knots. "Darn kids," he muttered to himself, "ain't right to treat us old folks the way they do," he said and managed to slip his right wrist free and then began untying himself. Once free, he hurried to the entrance of the cave, pushed the broken tree limbs away, and stepped out into the night. He studied the darkness with the eyes of an experienced woodsman and began walking down the trail.

"Freeze!" Conrad yelled and exploded up from behind the hood and ran at Mr. Rhodes.

"Hands in the air!" Sarah hollered, covering Conrad's rear. "Hands in the air!"

"Don't shoot!" Mr. Rhodes cried out and threw his arms shakily in the air.

Conrad ran up to Mr. Rhodes. "This isn't the kid," he

said in frustration. "With it being so dark, all I saw was a shadow—"

"Don't kick yourself," Sarah told Conrad. "All I saw was a shadow, too." Sarah focused on Mr. Rhodes, who was shaking all over like a leaf. "Mr. Rhodes, I'm Detective Garland and this is Detective Conrad Spencer."

Mr. Rhodes lowered his arms. "You two nearly scared the life out of me," he complained.

Sarah cast her eyes at the cave entrance and pulled Mr. Rhodes down beside the driver's door of the BMW, expecting gun fire to erupt from the cave at any second. "Sir, where is Don Street?"

Mr. Rhodes felt anguish permeate his mind. "Oh my, oh my," he said in a sorrowful tone. "I done went and let the snake go free to save my own hide."

"What do you mean?" Conrad insisted. "Sir, where is the kid?"

Mr. Rhodes shook his head. "All I wanted was a few fish for supper and look at the mess I done went and got myself into," he said in an exhausted voice.

"Please, sir, talk to us," Sarah pleaded.

"I told that snake about the old tunnel hidden under the big rock," Mr. Rhodes told Sarah and looked through the darkness into her face. "He was going to kill me, sure enough as I'm standing here, he was going to kill me. I had to try and save my life, now didn't I?"

"Go," Sarah yelled at Conrad.

Conrad shot to his feet and ran into the cave with his gun at the ready. A few minutes later, he ran back out. "There's a tunnel under the cave floor," he told Sarah. "Sir, where does that tunnel lead to?"

"Down to the river," Mr. Rhodes explained. "Tunnel twists and turns a bit...goes about a quarter of a mile...big enough for kids but mighty tight for an adult. That boy won't be moving at super speed."

Sarah looked at Conrad. "We have to hurry," she said in a quick voice. "Sir, what location at the river does the tunnel end?" she asked.

"Oh...if I remember right, close to the old swimming tree us kids used to play by in the old days," Mr. Rhodes explained. He pointed into the night. "Go that way until you hit the river and then follow the current down until you come upon a huge old tree with an old wooden swing tied up in its limbs...can't miss it...one of the biggest trees in the county and—" As Sarah and Conrad started to step away in the direction he indicated, Mr. Rhodes suddenly stopped talking and grabbed his chest. "My...my...heart..." he whimpered in a pained voice.

Conrad caught Mr. Rhodes in his arms and laid the old

man down on the ground. "Stay with us, sir," he said in a loud, stern voice. "We're going to get you help."

Mr. Rhodes didn't answer Conrad. Instead, he dropped into unconsciousness. "Call for help," Sarah begged Conrad and cast her eyes back into the darkness, "I'm going for Don."

Conrad wanted to argue but knew better. It was Sarah's unsolved case that had reared its ugly head from the past and this was now Sarah's killer to catch. The woman he was falling in love with needed this final closure. "Go... but know that...you're really taking over my heart," he said and looked at Sarah with worry. "Come back to me, okay?"

Sarah bent down and touched Conrad's cheek and then kissed his chin. "You're a good man, Conrad Spencer," she whispered and then ran off into the night, leaving Conrad behind.

"Okay, girl, let's focus and depend on your training," she urged her mind and cautiously worked a trail back to the river. When the sound of the river reached her ears, Sarah slowed down and eased forward through the night until she came to a steep embankment. She turned right and began following the current, working her way past trees, fallen logs and through bushes, feeling confident she would be able to reach Don in time.

The steep riverbank allowed her only a narrow ledge to pass by in some places, which was perilous in the dark. But then tragedy struck. The narrow spot Sarah ran on suddenly crumbled out from under her. "No!" Sarah cried out, throwing her arms forward in the hopes of grabbing a tree limb to stop her fall. But her hands came up empty and her body tumbled down a rough embankment and splashed into the river. Sarah felt her body sink down into a deep, dark, watery abyss of a pool in the river and then began kicking her legs. A few seconds later she emerged from the deep and began swimming toward the shoreline. As she did, a dark figure appeared above her.

"Well, well," Don growled and aimed his penlight and gun directly at Sarah. "What do we have here?"

Sarah stopped swimming and let her legs fall. She felt her feet barely touch the river's bottom but quickly pretended she was still treading water as her mind absorbed the hopeless situation. She was still gasping for breath after her fall. Don had the element of surprise and he was also holding the higher ground. "Don, give yourself up," she ordered, forcing her voice to remain calm and in control. She couldn't let Don know he was in control—keeping the killer's confidence shaken was vital.

"You cops and your drama," Don hissed down at Sarah. If

prison bars were his destiny than he would take Sarah down with him. She had defied him, betrayed him, and now if he was caught in this manhunt, he would never get the right people back in their places to solve his father's murder, as he still desperately hoped would be possible.

Besides, killing a cop, he thought in his sick mind, was far different than killing an old man. Who knows, maybe he might be hailed as a hero in prison for whacking the world-famous Detective Garland, the woman who single-handedly took down the Back Alley Killer. Sure, Don thought, as his hideous murderous rage resurfaced, he'd be a hero and who knows, maybe someone might make a movie about him. Everyone would know his name.

"Don, don't make matters worse for yourself," Sarah replied desperately, wondering how fast she could swing her right hand out of the river and get a clean shot at Don. Not fast enough, she lamented, staring at the gun Don was aiming at her. Don had admitted to being a horrible shot—and maybe his words were true—but Sarah didn't want to risk being fired upon at such a close distance. "Don—"

"Shut up!" Don yelled at Sarah. "I told you, you're going down, cop! You think I'm scared by your little manhunt? No way. After I kill you, I'll be famous! If I land in prison, I'll be a hero! Even if killing you means a harsher punishment, I don't care...you have to die!"

"The way your father died?" Sarah asked Don.

Don snarled, his insane face contorting like a furious viper preparing to spit acidic poison at Sarah. "Don't you ever mention my dad's name...ever!"

"Your father was practicing a very dangerous stunt, wasn't he?" Sarah asked, playing for time. "He didn't see you arrive. When you called out to him, you caught him by surprise, he tripped, got the ropes he was working with tangled around his body, and fell off the roof."

"Shut up!" Don yelled and fired a bullet blindly at Sarah. The bullet flew wide and right into the water, safely missing Sarah. "Shut up! You don't know nothing, cop!"

Sarah steadied her nerves and prepared to take a shot at Don. "You saw your father die, Don. And you blamed yourself. But then you blocked out the nightmare you witnessed and convinced yourself someone else killed your father, didn't you?"

"Shut up!" Don yelled and fired a second bullet at Sarah. The bullet struck the river again and vanished, missing Sarah. "You're nothing but a stupid cop who failed to solve my dad's case."

"How could I have solved the case, Don, when your mother forced J&P Brothers to make everyone at the studio clam up on me?" Sarah asked. The last thing she wanted was to continue playing a panicked round of target practice with Don. Sooner or later one of the bullets might hit her. "I know that your mother rigged the books for J&P Brothers, Don. I know she covered up your father's death with a lie and claimed he was murdered, when in fact his death was accidental."

"I didn't kill my dad!" Don yelled and prepared to empty the clip in his gun at Sarah. "You shut your stupid mouth, cop! I didn't kill my dad...my mom, she found the real killer...I killed him...and you...you were supposed to come back and solve the murder...I had it all planned out!"

"Until Rebecca caused you a problem," Sarah said and then stopped talking when she saw movement behind Don. Someone was sneaking up behind him through the darkness. Sarah forced calmness to her mind and continued. "Don, you killed an innocent woman. You killed an innocent man who you only thought had murdered your father. How many people have to die?"

"Only you," Don roared and steadied his gun. "I'm going to kill you if it's the last thing I do. If I'm caught then I'm caught, but Canada isn't too far away. If I'm smart and stay hidden, I should be safe to cross the border," he said, furiously shaking as the gun aimed at Sarah's head.

"I don't think so," a voice said. "You might pollute the land."

"Huh?" Don said and spun around. He was met with a fierce punch to the jaw. The impact caused him to stumble backward, dazed. Don began madly flailing his arms in an attempt to steady his balance. But as he did, his attacker lunged forward and landed a kick solidly in his stomach. Don's body collapsed to the ground and rolled down the slope toward the river. But instead of hitting the water, his head struck a rock lodged in the mud on the river's edge.

The last thing Don remembered before his world went black was wondering who hit him. Whoever took him by surprise wasn't a man. Then the darkness took him and he saw and thought nothing more.

Amanda perched her hands on her hips and shook her head, looking down at Sarah. "Well," she said, looking like the warmest shadow Sarah had ever seen in her life, "it's a good thing Harry came to sit with Nate, huh? Otherwise, I might still be at the hospital."

Sarah felt a huge smile sweep over her face. "June Bug, you are my hero," she called out as she hurried to wade out of the river and went over to Don. "He's out cold," she said and sat down on a fallen tree limb. Amanda made her way down to the river's edge and sat down next to her best friend. Sarah put her soaking wet arm around Amanda and hugged her shoulder. "My hero."

"Remember that when you pay for my shopping spree," Amanda smiled and hugged Sarah back, even though her best friend was coated in mud and dripping with river water. Then she looked down at Don. "Another monster," she said and shook her head in disgust. "Los

Angeles, the next time we go on a trip together, remind me to have my head examined, okay?"

"Deal," Sarah promised and then jumped to her feet when she heard someone running up to the river.

"Sarah?" Conrad called out in a worried voice.

"Down here," Sarah called back.

Conrad made his way down to the river, spotted Amanda, and then saw Don's limp form at the river's edge. He slowed and simply shoved his hands into the pockets of his leather jacket. "I guess you girls have everything under control. I better get back to the old man," he said, pulled a pair of handcuffs from his right jacket pocket, and tossed them down next to Don. "The ambulance is on the way for Mr. Rhodes, I have to get back. Cuff him, partner," he said with a wink and walked away.

"You bet...partner," Sarah smiled.

Amanda raised her eyebrows, grinned, and didn't say a word. Instead, she helped Sarah handcuff Don and drag his body away from the river's edge. Sure, she thought, being friends with Sarah Garland was risky, but no one could want a better friend.

Nate sat down at his kitchen table and eyed Conrad. "What's the matter, cabbage soup too hot for you?"

"No," Conrad said with a red face, "cabbage soup...just fine," he finished and dived for his glass of tea.

Sarah shared a grin with Amanda. They were eating delicious warm bowls of pinto beans and cornbread. "Nate, how are you feeling?" she asked, turning her attention away from Conrad for the moment.

Nate looked at Sarah and Amanda. He smiled to see both women looking so pretty in the sunflower yellow dresses that looked like the same style that his wife once wore. The girls, who were leaving the following morning, had picked the dresses to wear for him as a special gift. "Old Nate is just fine," Nate promised. "You heard that fancy doctor. Only thing wrong with me is my old cancer. My body let go of me the other day at the courthouse because I was running too hard, that's all."

Sarah reached out and patted Nate's hand. "We're going to get through your cancer together," she promised.

"Old Nate leaves his cancer up to God," Nate smiled at Sarah. "When it's my time, it'll be my time. Besides, my wife is waiting for me and I'm sure anxious to see her again and tell her about you girls. Of course, my wife has been watching the whole time and probably kicking up a fuss over you."

Amanda took a bite of beans. Her heart felt sad. The last

thing in the world she wanted to do was say goodbye to Nate. She had come to love the old man very deeply. "I can stay with you a while," she offered.

"You got a husband waiting for you," Nate told Amanda and patted her hand. "Old Nate will be just fine."

Conrad looked across the kitchen table into Nate's eyes. The old man still had some good years left to him, he saw. "Now, ladies. The last thing a man like Mr. Ringgold wants or needs is two women sticking around and babying him every day. He's an independent man who knows his way in life," Conrad said, feeling a warm respect and admiration for the man. He turned to Nate. "We'd still like to visit you, if that's okay."

"Sure, sure," Nate assured Conrad and pointed at his bowl of cabbage soup. "Eat up, son. Don't let your cabbage go and get cold on you. Old Nate don't like cold cabbage. Cold cabbage is a crime. Cabbage is meant to be eaten right out of the pot."

Conrad winced, lifted a bite of cabbage soup to his mouth, and gobbled it down. His face turned red as a chili pepper. "Good," he said with tears pooling in the corners of his eyes. "Kinda hot...a little heavy on the cayenne, but good."

"Cayenne is good for the heart," Nate replied and winked at Sarah and Amanda. "So, you girls are going to Los Angeles after you leave here, huh?"

"I still want to see Pete," Sarah admitted. "And I promised to take Amanda on an all-expenses paid shopping trip."

Amanda grinned from ear to ear. "Ah, the price us selfless heroes have to pay to get some recognition."

Conrad rolled his eyes. He adored Amanda but he knew that the woman was definitely going to milk her hero status for all it was worth—or at least until his wallet was empty and Sarah's credit card was drained. "I'm chipping in on the shopping trip," he told Nate.

Amanda nodded. "Yes, kind sir, you are. But not to worry," Amanda said and threw her right hand over and up to her forehead. "Alas, this fair maiden will only shop in the most expensive clothing shops and eat at the most luxurious restaurants and sleep on the softest beds."

Conrad winced. "Really?" he asked in a painful voice.

Amanda lowered her hand and laughed. "No, love, not really. I called my dear husband this morning and he has ordered me home. It seems he misses me too much. It looks like you and my dear friend are going to Los Angeles alone. Well, not completely alone." Amanda looked at the back door where Mittens was lapping up a warm bowl of milk.

Sarah slowly put down the spoon she was holding and folded her arms. "You know...as much as I want to see Pete, I think I would rather pass and go home, myself. I miss Pete, but right now he's going to be busy tying this case up. I'll get down to Los Angeles and see him another time, or he can fly up and stay a week with me at the cabin like he's always promised. Besides," she said, looking at Mittens, "my baby girl is getting homesick."

Conrad felt relief settle into his chest. He knew Pete was just a friend of Sarah's, but he couldn't help but be pleased that she was coming home to Alaska and not spending the week visiting her old stomping grounds in Los Angeles. "I'll return the SUV to the rental car agency and we can drive back together."

"Sounds good," Sarah smiled at Conrad.

Nate saw a warm glow enter Sarah's eyes every time she looked at Conrad. Love was in the air. But the love he saw forming in Sarah toward her man wasn't a love that needed to be rushed. The love in Sarah's eyes was a sweet, honest, patient love that needed nurturing a bit. "Well," he said and turned his mind to Don for a minute, "what is going to come of this mess before you three drive back up to Alaska tomorrow?"

Sarah unfolded her arms. "Don Street," she said and picked her spoon up again, "has confessed to the killings. But he's pleading insanity, saying that seeing his father die caused him to go insane...and maybe that's half true. But a boy like Don, the murderous intent I saw in his eyes, he would have grown up to be—"

"The next Back Alley Killer?" Conrad finished for Sarah. "You ladies could have stopped a future serial killer in his tracks."

The thought of Don growing up to become a serial killer sent cold chills down Sarah's back. "I'm just thankful this case ended well and that we're all safe." Sarah turned her head and looked at Amanda. "Thanks to you, June Bug. You're always saving me."

"Well, someone has to," Amanda teased Sarah, then she grew somber. "When I heard the gunshots, I panicked. And then I heard that crazy kid yelling at you. I...well, I wasn't very brave. I acted out of...well, fear rather than courage, love. I was scared that snake might hear me sneaking up on him, turn around, and shoot me."

"You did just fine," Conrad assured Amanda. "You always do."

Amanda nibbled on a bite of beans. "Guys, can we not tell my dear husband about any of this? If he finds out that I slugged a killer in the face he might not ever let me leave the cabin again."

"Deal," Sarah promised, laughing. Then they heard someone knock on the back door.

"Door is unlocked, but watch the puppy," Nate called out.

Paul opened the back door and stepped inside the

kitchen. Harry followed behind, holding a deck of Uno cards in his right hand. "Nate," Paul said and nodded, "Detective Garland."

"Sheriff Bufford, how are you?" Sarah asked.

"Retiring," Paul replied with a deep sigh of relief and closed the door behind him. He looked down at the puppy and then back at Sarah. Mittens wasn't in any mood to be bothered. All she wanted was her warm milk and her momma's lap. "I heard that you're leaving Prate tomorrow?"

"Yes, we're driving back to Alaska," Sarah explained. "I was going to stop by the courthouse and say goodbye."

"Don't bother," Paul replied. "I've cleared out my office and turned in my badge."

"What in the world for?" Nate fussed.

"Because I was a coward," Paul said and held his head down in shame. "I failed my wife, I failed the good people of Prate...and I failed myself."

"Oh, you're acting like a big dummy," Nate retorted. "You got scared over your wife, that's all. I would have acted the same way you did, Paul."

"Already told him that," Harry said and studied the kitchen table. He spotted the cabbage soup. "Mind if I have some cabbage, Nate?"

"Why ask a silly question? My house is your house, you old fart," Nate groused at Harry and pointed to an empty chair. "Sit down and eat. We'll play Uno shortly." Harry sat himself down, grabbed a green bowl, and ladled out some cabbage. "Paul," Nate continued, "if you go retiring because you feel ashamed of yourself, then you'll go 'round kicking yourself for the rest of your years."

"I can't forgive myself for betraying my badge over a threat from some stupid kid," Paul argued.

"Don Street was a killer, Sheriff," Sarah pointed out. "Maybe his appearance was that of a kid, but his mind was that of an evil killer."

"I've seen ten-year-olds walk into gang fights with guns," Conrad added. "Sheriff, you got spooked because Don Street threatened your wife. It happens."

"I appreciate your kind words," Paul said and walked back to the kitchen door. "I wanted to come back and say goodbye in person. I'm taking my wife away from Prate for a little while. We need time to figure out whether we want to remain living here or move away."

"Now, Paul—" Nate began to object.

Paul held up his hand. "You folks have a good night," he said and slipped out of the back door.

"That poor man," Amanda said and shook her head. "He's sure beating himself up about this."

"Yep," Harry said and began working on his cabbage. "But don't worry about Paul. In time, he'll come around to the truth and settle his insides."

Sarah wasn't so certain Harry was right. Paul's eyes told her that the man would never forgive himself for betraying his badge and the people of Prate. But what could she do? Paul Bufford would have to reckon with the consequences of his own choices to remain in a job that he had not fully believed in, and perhaps that was important. The truth was, she was so homesick and anxious to sleep in her own bed that she had trouble focusing on Paul's problems. "I guess Don Street had another victim, one he's not aware of," she said.

"Yep," Nate said and took a sip of coffee. "Well, no sense in worrying over Paul when supper is before us. Keep telling Old Nate the scoop, Sarah."

Sarah took a drink of tea. "Don Street confessed that he saw his father die. The death happened the way I theorized it did and his mother confirmed it. Don's father was working on a roof, preparing a stunt, when Don called out his name from the ground. Don said his father startled some, tripped on the ropes he had on the roof, and...well, you guys can figure out the rest." Sarah put down her tea. "Bonnie Street confessed to covering up the death and making it appear like murder or an accidental death in order to protect her son. And because she had been rigging the books for J&P Brothers, she tossed around a few threats that forced J&P Brothers to keep their employees silent."

Nate shook his head. "My, my," he grunted, "the messes this old world has going on in it sure are enough to keep an old man awake at night."

"Tell me about it," Harry agreed. "It's getting to where I'm almost ready to start locking my back door at night."

"Almost ready?" Amanda asked. "You mean you don't lock your doors at all?"

"Nah," Harry said and filled his mouth full of cabbage, "never saw a need to. I don't like being scared in my own home."

"You better believe it," Nate said and scratched his head. "Ain't fitting for a man to be scared when he lays down his head to sleep at night."

The kitchen grew silent. Sarah looked into Nate's face. The old man was staring at his back door. Finally, Amanda spoke. "Well, my sweet loves," she said to everyone, "when are we going to play Uno? I don't see any sense in letting the outside world ruin our night together." Amanda pointed at the back door. "Outside that door, there are plenty of ugly people roaming around like snakes and there's not a thing in the world any one of us sitting in this kitchen can do about it. All we can do is trust in the Lord and handle one day at a time. So, with that said, I'm going to check on the brownies I have baking and Harry, you start shuffling those Uno cards."

Sarah looked at Amanda with admiration. "Well said, June Bug."

Amanda winked at Sarah and then smiled at Conrad. "Uh, love, your cabbage soup is getting cold."

Conrad looked down at his cabbage soup, grimaced, and then took a bite. "Nate...maybe not so much cayenne pepper next time."

Mittens finished her milk, padded over to Sarah, and began whining. "Okay, baby," Sarah smiled and picked Mittens up into her arms. "I think my baby has to go outside. I'll be back in a few minutes."

Sarah walked Mittens outside and set her down in the fresh grass and raised her head up at the night sky. She saw a breathtaking canvas filled with endless twinkling stars over her head. For a while, she pushed the thought of Don Street from her thoughts and listened to the beautiful silence of the night as she stared up at the heavens. "The world can be very ugly," she whispered, "but the world can also be very beautiful. All we can do is take it one day at a time, right Mittens?" Mittens snuggled up next to Sarah's legs and let out a sweet little bark. "That's right, baby. Now," she said and picked Mittens up, "let's forget all about our problems and have a peaceful night." Sarah walked Mittens back inside and settled down for a cozy night of Uno and coffee, contented and safe.

But far away, a daring prison escape was taking place. Soon Sarah was going to meet a monster that had never forgotten about her in his dreams.

ABOUT THE AUTHOR

Wendy Meadows is an emerging author of cozy mysteries. She lives in "The Granite State" with her husband, two sons, two cats and lovable Labradoodle.

When she isn't working on her stories she likes to tend to her flowers, relax with her pets and play video games with her family.

Get in Touch with Wendy
www.wendymeadows.com

amazon.com/author/wendymeadows

goodreads.com/wendymeadows

bookbub.com/authors/wendy-meadows

facebook.com/AuthorWendyMeadows

twitter.com/wmeadowscozy

Maple Hills Cozy Mystery Series

Nether Edge Mystery Series

Chocolate Cozy Mystery Series

Alaska Cozy Mystery Series

Sweet Peach Bakery Cozy Series

Sweetfern Harbor Mystery Series

Made in the USA
Middletown, DE
06 September 2021

47723091R00113